MY SWEETEST OBSESSION

THE SWEETEST LIE DUET
BOOK 2

GWYN MCNAMEE

MY SWEETEST OBSESSION
© 2025 Gwyn McNamee

Cover Model: Jerrin; Photographer: Wander Aguiar

Cover Design: BlueSky Design

Editing: Stephie Walls at Wallflower Edits

To anyone who ever faced unexpected consequences and still found the light in the darkness...

TRIGGER WARNING

The Sweetest Lie duet contains many elements that may
be triggering for some individuals (some of these
elements will also be plot spoilers). Please visit my website
to check the detailed trigger list here:
www.gwynmcnamee.com/thesweetestlieduet
triggerwarnings

1

CAM

Agony ten times worse than any withdrawal symptoms I've ever suffered sears through me, gutting me open and flaying me alive with the knowledge that I have to come clean now.

There is no more hiding what I've done.

My vision blurs, hot tears filling my eyes as the alcohol burns in my gut. "I have two things to tell you." The first one pulls my lips into a sad smile because this is the worst possible time, the worst possible place, the worst possible circumstances to be saying it. "One will make you hate me; the other...will make you despise me."

Ivy's tear-filled eyes narrow on me, consumed with so much confusion and concern—and a warmth I never thought I would see there after I told her the truth behind what had caused my rift with Drew.

I never believed she could forgive me for what I did, and the time I've gotten to spend with her, the past few nights, was more than I ever deserved.

Even after everything I just told her, she still cares so much it fucking hurts because I'm the last person she should care about, the last person she should be feeling anything for but hate.

She sets down the doll and starts to push to her feet. "I could *never* hate you, let alone *despise* you, Cam."

I want so badly to believe her, to be able to luxuriate in the fact that *this* woman feels so much for me that *she* believes it when she says it.

But it isn't real.

Her declaration is only made because she doesn't understand. She doesn't *know* the depths of my depravity or what it cost both of us.

Holding up my hand to stop her from coming to me, I shake my head as a sob tears from my chest. My next sharp breath draws her honeysuckle scent into my lungs, making this a thousand times more painful. "You don't know what I've done."

She clutches her fists to her chest, confusion furrowing her brow as she shakes her head, sending her dark hair floating around her. "There's nothing you ever could have done that I can't forgive, Cam."

Those words are another twist of the knife driven into my heart today, the one that's left me wounded and bleeding out here on the floor, desperate enough to find a way to end the pain that I resorted to things I swore I would never touch again.

I offer her a sad smile, knowing what she said isn't true. Some things are unforgivable, even for someone whose soul is as beautiful and generous as Ivy's, and this is one of them, which makes this confession a thousand times harder. "I've been in love with you since the moment I first laid eyes on you..."

Finally saying those words should be a relief.

I've waited so long to tell her. Held it inside for *years* while I tried to drown those feelings any way I could—with booze, drugs, women. Seeking out *anything* to kill that soul-deep *need* for the woman I only met once, who I barely knew, who I *shouldn't* want. Because it had already cost me Drew, and I knew it was costing me so much more each time I shoved a needle into my arm.

But all I feel is agony that even the copious amount of whiskey I've drunk can't alleviate.

Ivy's brow furrows, soft eyes searching my face for some explanation she won't find there because she could never guess something this horrific. "Why would I hate you for that?"

Because it ruined everything.

Because it's why we're here *like* this—both suffering.

Because it's why Drew isn't here.

"Because"—I heave in a breath, tears falling down my cheeks in endless waves—"it makes the second thing seem...calculated."

Ivy trembles, still kneeling in front of me, the damn G.I. Joe lying on the floor between us as if Drew himself is sitting here and waiting for me to finally confess *every-thing.* Fear now coats her gaze, mixed with the other emotions I saw earlier. "You're scaring me..."

Good.

Finally.

All the warnings I've given her to stay away, assurances

that she wants nothing to do with me or my life, will finally make sense.

Because it's time she knows the truth.

All of it.

"You should be scared, Ivy." I swallow thickly, forcing down the ball of emotion clogging my throat, but it refuses to budge. "Because I'm the reason Drew is dead. I killed him."

Ivy recoils at my statement.

Her already pale skin goes ashen as she drops back on her haunches. What I wouldn't give to know the true color of it or of those expressive eyes that hold so many emotions all the time. Drew's description of her from before I went and blew everything up allow me to *try* to visualize it, but after so many years of only seeing black, white, and varying shades of gray, his description of peachy skin that darkens when she blushes and amber eyes that sparkle with flecks of gold doesn't mean a whole lot to me.

The only color I really remember is red.

The color *she* made me see again.

"What?" Those perfect lips I've kissed and tasted and loved so much open and close a few times as she shakes her head. "What the hell are you talking about, Cam?"

I clench my jaw in a fight against another sob threatening to climb out of my throat.

I've known agonizing pain in my life.

Physical.

Emotional.

The kind of soul-crushing torment that leaves lasting scars.

Yet, having to look at Ivy and say all of this is ten thousand times worse than anything else I've suffered.

I knew I would eventually have to tell her, that I'd have to come clean, that I'd have to confess everything; I just thought I'd have more time. That there'd be a better way to do it, a less painful way for her, for both of us.

But I was wrong.

There is no way to explain that I killed Drew without crushing her completely. And watching her face crumple at my words, hearing her confusion over my admission, I know she won't ever recover from this.

She was barely hanging on as it was after losing him, and any lifeline she thought I gave her was just cut, leaving her floating alone on that dark water where we spread his ashes.

And there's no way for me to reel her back, to get her back on solid ground.

All I'm going to do is push her farther under the roiling waves.

Holding her gaze while I tell her this makes the alcohol threaten to come back up, but I swallow it back. "I told you I thought the wedding invitation was from him, that it was him gloating that you were *his*." My hand tightens around the bottle at the memory of receiving it. "It pissed me the fuck off. It's why I came back..."

Ivy narrows her eyes, so much uncertainty in them that they can't seem to focus on me. "I...thought you came back because Drew died."

I shake my head, refusing to look away from her, even if it would be so much easier if I did. "No, Ivy. I came back for *you*." More tears slide down my cheeks. "It's *always* been about *you*."

Her entire body trembles, her skin taking on an unmissable deathly pallor that's evident even without the benefit of seeing its true color.

"When my mom told me that Drew had proposed to you..." All those feelings rush back—the anger, the jealousy that gave me an irrational ire toward him simply because she loved him. "It made me realize I couldn't live without you. It made me understand that I had to get my shit together if I had *any* hope of ever having a chance with you." I give her a sad smile. "It's why I went to rehab, Ivy. Because I knew I was a mess, and I wanted to be the person you met that night, not"—I wave my free hand over myself, the bottle, and the drugs lying beside me— "*this*."

She buries her face in her hands. "I don't understand, Cam. I—"

"I didn't come back because Drew died. I've been back in Philly for almost six months, Ivy."

Her back stiffens, her hands falling away to reveal her wide eyes and trembling lips. "What?"

I motion toward the box. "The invitation came, I don't know, a week or so after you mailed it, and I was so fucking pissed." Shoving my free hand through my hair, I shake my head. "I couldn't stop thinking about you and what had happened that night and how he was shoving it in my face that he got you. And I said 'fuck it' and flew home with every intention of fighting for you, of telling you that it was me in the garden before you could make a huge mistake and marry him."

She presses her hands over her chest as I take another drink and let the bottle dangle from my fingertips. I stare at it. That familiar dark liquid that has always been my favorite now makes me want to vomit, but I can't stop drinking it.

"But I had barely been clean for six months then, and one of the things they tell is in rehab and in NA is that getting into a relationship during that first year of sobriety isn't a good idea." I lift my gaze to meet hers. "Because people replace the high from drugs with that intense emotion and euphoria of a new relationship. So...I waited..."

"You've been *here* for six months?"

Six. Long. Agonizing. Months.

I nod, watching her struggle to process what I'm telling her.

"But—"

"I didn't tell anyone." I take another drink, hoping maybe *this* one will tip me over that line and into finally feeling nothing. "I just bided my time...and watched you."

Her mouth falls open. "You...*watched* me?"

A sad smile pulls at my lips, remembering all those times I sat outside her house or the garden center, waiting to catch even a glimpse of her. "I couldn't stay away." I let my shoulders rise and fall. "And the day I hit a year, I called Drew..." My heart lodges in my throat, and I gulp to clear it. "I told him that I was planning to approach you, to tell you what happened, and that I was in love with you. And he flipped. This place"—I motion around us—"was where I lived before I moved back to London. I rented it out to other people while I was gone. But no one was occupying it at the time I came back, so he knew where to find me..." I take another long drink of liquid courage I'm going to need to finish telling her this story. "He came here that same night I called to confront me."

Shaking hands clenched in her lap, Ivy watches me with tears streaming down her cheeks. "What night?"

Her voice breaks because she already knows the answer.

I can see it in the darkness creeping into her gaze.

Choking back a sob, I force myself to say the words I know will destroy her. "The night he died. One year to the day I got clean..."

Her mouth falls open on a silent gasp, and she scans the loft as if she's going to see evidence of something. "Wh-what *happened*, Cam?"

"We argued."

I take a sip of the whiskey, letting the burn of the alcohol down my throat warm my gut, when my entire body has felt ice cold since the minute I opened that box from Drew.

No amount of alcohol is going to relieve that.

Nor will the drugs sitting beside me that I've been fighting with myself over for the last several hours.

I knew that when I called my old dealer. I knew it when I opened the door for him and took it. I knew it when I popped open this bottle and took my first swig.

But I was so desperate not to feel that I did it anyway.

The only thing that's kept me from sticking that needle in my vein has been how badly my hand shakes each time I try to pick it up, and my sponsor Dale's words echoing in my head, telling me not to do it.

I rest my forearm on my knee and let the bottle dangle between them. "I told him he was an asshole for sending me what he sent me..."

Ivy's hand flies over her mouth, and her eyes dart to the package on the floor at the G.I. Joe doll lying at her knees. His peace offering. An olive branch. "Oh, God, no..."

She knows.

She understands the ramifications of what I said to him.

How everything got so twisted.

My eyes drift to the doll, too. "Of course, I didn't know he had sent *that*. I was referring to the invitation." The one *she* sent. "He flew off the handle like I've never seen him before. We were screaming at each other, and I told him that you deserved to know the truth before you two got married."

Her tears flow freely down her cheeks, and she struggles to swallow. "Wh-what did he say?"

The corner of my mouth quirks up, despite me fighting it. "He said I was ruining everything, but that it wouldn't matter, because you would choose him. But he was scared. I could see it in his eyes. And I was happy he was scared because I was so pissed...about something that, turns out, wasn't even true."

She shoves her trembling hands through her hair, tightening her grip on it. "Oh, God..."

I finger the bottle, brushing my thumb across the lip. "I was brutal. I was ruthless. I let my anger take over, and I told him the only reason the two of you ever ended up together was because of me, and once you knew the truth, you'd call off the wedding. He told me to go to hell and left."

"Wh-where was he going?"

His words that night still ringing in my ears as if he had just said them, I offer her a half-shrug. "I assume home to you to try to cut me off at the pass and tell you everything before I could."

Her entire body shakes violently as she waits for what she must know is coming, and I have to muster up all the courage I have to get the words out, including some more of the liquid variety.

I chug the whiskey, wincing this time as my head spins from the alcohol now coursing through my bloodstream. My vision blurs staring at the mostly empty bottle. "As soon as he left, I felt terrible about it. I ran out after him, but he had already pulled away from the curb, and there was no way I was going to catch him on foot." I release a little snort. "I even tried running after him for the first block or two, but he wasn't stopping for me. He was driving like a bat outta hell..."

I raise my eyes to meet hers.

It's all I need to do to confirm what happened.

"Oh, God." She presses her hand over her heart as a hiccupped sob steals her breath. "The stop sign he ran..."

I nod slowly. "Two miles from here."

"Oh, my God." Ivy sucks in a sharp inhale as her chest starts rising and falling rapidly. "Oh, God. Oh, God. Oh, God."

She repeats the words over and over and over, then covers her mouth with her hand and gags.

"Shit, Ivy—" I try to push up, but the room spins

violently, and I crumple back onto the floor. My head slams back against the bricks again, and I squeeze my eyes closed long enough to get the world to stop its rotation, then open them.

Ivy turns away from me and crawls to the wastebasket next to the kitchen island and dry heaves over it.

I shift up to attempt to get to my feet again, but she holds out a hand to me.

"Don't. You. Come. *Near*. Me."

Her words are like another sharp slice from the knife lodged in my heart, but I drop back onto my ass and let my head fall against the bricks. This time, the sharp bite of pain is more than welcome. It isn't anywhere near what I deserve. "I told you that you would hate me."

"Did you—" She heaves again, gasping for air as she tries to gain control of her body. Her hands tremble, clutching the edges of the wastebasket, her eyes clench closed, and her lips quiver. She finally glances over at me. "Did you know he was in the accident?"

I shake my head "No." Tears burn my eyes, blurring my vision of her, and I swallow back another sob. "I was going to call him to apologize the next day. Give him some time to cool off, but then my mom called that night..."

Ivy heaves again as I fight the desire to do the same fucking thing.

Reliving that moment, hearing Mom say those words and knowing I had caused it—all of it threatens to drag me even deeper into the dark abyss of despair I've already dived into tonight.

"It was my fault, Ivy, all of it. I killed Drew. If I hadn't kissed you that night, if I hadn't come back, if I hadn't fought with him, if I hadn't said those things and made him leave that angry, he'd still be here. Everything would be how it's supposed to be. He'd still be alive, you two would be married, and I'd be back in London..."

Ivy settles back on her ass and leans against the kitchen counter, watching me warily, her face pale and clammy looking. She wipes her mouth with the back of her arm as her tears continue to roll down her cheeks.

The way she looks at me—like I'm a complete stranger instead of the man she's been sharing a bed with—destroys what's left of my heart. That knife so deeply embedded in it finally tears away the final pieces so that *nothing* is left except my guilt and agony.

I swallow back the desire to beg her forgiveness because there's no way to ask for that from her.

Not with what I've done.

What I've caused.

"Did you go back to London?"

There it is.

At some point, she was going to realize it was a full month after Drew died before I showed up on her doorstep, and she was bound to want an explanation. It's the least she deserves.

I shake my head. "No. When my mom called and said he had died, and I realized what I had done"—I take a sharp inhale and chug on the bottle again, taking several long swallows and hissing at the burn—"I couldn't leave her." I meet Ivy's gaze. "I couldn't leave *you.*"

"But—" She shakes her head. "You didn't come to the funeral. Your mother says she hasn't seen you in years. I don't..."

I press my lips together, trying to control the emotions warring inside me. Ivy needs answers, but the more I give her, the worse I feel. The more confident I become that there will never be an end to this torment. "I couldn't face her knowing what I had done, that I was the reason she had lost Drew. I couldn't face you, but I made sure you were both okay as much as I could."

Her brow furrows again as she narrows her eyes on me. "What do you mean?" After a few seconds, her eyes widen slightly. "Why did you come to my house that night —that *specific* night?"

I suck in a deep breath and release a heavy sigh. "Because it was supposed to be your wedding day. I watched you sign for that delivery, and I knew what it was because my mom told me they were supposed to be delivered that weekend. I knew it was his ashes, and I knew it was undoubtedly the most excruciating day of your life. I had already seen how distraught you were, and I was worried about you. I wanted to—"

Shit.

It doesn't matter what I wanted to do that night or any other time.

None of it matters.

Nothing will *ever* make this okay for her.

She bolts back up onto her knees and heaves over the trash can again, tears dripping down her face as her body revolts against the information I'm giving her.

And that need to explain, even if it doesn't mean anything, overwhelms me.

"I needed to make sure you and my mom were all right, but I couldn't tell you guys what I had done. What had happened. I couldn't—" I choke on a sob. "You asked me why I ordered a beer at the bar, if it was to test myself." I shake my head. "I don't do it to test myself, Ivy. I do it to *torture* myself because I *deserve* it. I deserve every ounce of agony I suffer staring at that pint of beer or double shot of whiskey sitting on the table or bar in front of me. I deserve it because it is *nothing* compared to what he suffered in his last moments...because of me. Because *I* was selfish. Because *I* wanted something that wasn't mine. Because *I* took a taste of it, knowing I shouldn't and *couldn't* have it. I sit and stare at that drink I can't have to remind myself what one *taste* of you cost me."

She whips her head toward me, and the pain and hatred in her eyes are enough to make me recoil. "I thought he was having an *affair*."

I clench my hand around the bottle. "I didn't know you would think that. I had no idea. I would've told you sooner if I had—"

"Fuck you, Camden."

With her body trembling, she rights herself and struggles to stand, grabbing the counter to keep herself steady.

"Ivy, please—"

I somehow climb to my own unsteady feet, hand pressed to the brick wall to keep myself from tumbling over. The whole room spins, her beautiful face a black and white and gray kaleidoscope. I squeeze my eyes closed until it stops. When I reopen them, she's already on the move toward the door.

Doing exactly what I knew she would when she found out the truth, leaving me without a look back.

"Ivy, please, I'm so sorry." A strangled, desperate sob slips out. "I—"

She stops and whirls to face me, her hands fisted at her sides. "You don't get to apologize to me. This is all your fault, Cam, *all* of it. You took Drew from me. You tainted my memory of him, of what we had. All for *what*? So you could prove that you could *take* me? What kind of sick fucking game is that? One I want *no* part of but you put me at the center of it anyway."

Her steps move her toward the door, but then she pauses for a moment and turns. A second passes where I can physically *feel* her hatred, rage, and anguish rolling off her. Then she stalks toward me and bends to scoop up the needle and heroin that have been sitting beside me for hours. With her eyes locked on me, she closes the final few steps between us and snatches the bottle from my hand.

With it clenched tightly in her trembling fist, she eyes it and then her gaze drifts to the drugs in her other hand. "But I'm also not going to be responsible for you killing yourself."

She turns and storms out the still-open loft door.

Her heavy footsteps on the metal staircase ring in my ears as I slide back down the brick, not even caring about how it bites and scrapes my bare skin.

I thought losing Drew was going to kill me.

But I was wrong.

It's this.

Seeing how badly I destroyed Ivy and obliterated everything good in her life.

Losing her is what's truly going to do it.

2

IVY

I thought I knew darkness.

I believed I had lived in it after Drew's death and become old friends with that place in my head where nothing and no one could penetrate the gloom.

I understood it, had even embraced it at times.

It became familiar.

Just the new way life was going to be.

Yet what sucks me in now is something new.

An inky blackness so thick, so heavy it steals my vision, my breath, my soul.

Pure, impenetrable onyx.

I should be fighting it.

At least *attempting* to swim and struggle against the riptide of anguish that wants to consume me and drag me down to those inescapable depths.

But I don't have it in me anymore.

I've fought too hard for too long to stay afloat.

Those obsidian waves that finally tugged Drew away from me can take me now, too.

As long as they bring me to him.

Because there is no light left.

No hope.

Nothing to keep me from embracing that which I've battled for months.

It was all a lie.

An obsession that led to this agony.

3

CAM

The smell of coffee and harsh sunlight falling on my face jerk me awake.

A sledgehammer instantly pounds against my temples.

I release an agonized groan, rolling to the side of my bed, my stomach immediately roiling badly enough that I fight to swallow back bile that threatens to make me heave.

Fuck.

A heavy cloud of pain and regret envelops me, and I try to bury my head under my pillow to keep out the world longer so I don't have to remember how I got into this state.

Because it's bad.

Very bad.

I haven't felt like this in so long that I forgot how awful it can really get.

Fuuuuuuuck...

My brain refuses to fire. It just flat-out declines to get on board with this whole waking up thing, but my gut continues to revolt, making me choke back its contents rather than have to leave bed to crawl to the bathroom and retch. Which I apparently did already at least once, given the taste in my dry mouth.

Something clangs across the loft in the direction of the kitchen, and I finally lift my head from beneath the pillow to attempt an investigation.

I freeze, both because my stomach doesn't appreciate the movement, nor does my head, but also because Mom stands at the counter, pouring coffee out of the carafe into two mugs.

What the fuck?

Squeezing my eyes closed, I reopen them in case I'm hallucinating, but she's still there.

Her eyes flick over to me, and she presses her lips together in a firm line, giving me "the look" I always dreaded as a child—the one that screams *disappointed*, which is far worse than her *mad* look. "About time you woke up."

"Mom?"

The word comes scratchy from my raw throat, as if it, too, can't believe she's here in my studio.

How the fuck?

I struggle to remember anything about how she got here...

But all I see is *her*.

Bits and pieces of my conversation with Ivy flash through my head so rapidly that it makes the room spin again and my nausea exponentially worse. But not because of my epic hangover. The roiling in my stomach comes from what I *can* remember...

I cringe, squeezing my eyes closed, and drop back into the bed, releasing another groan as I curl in on myself, pressing my hands over my revolting gut. But that sweet floral smell still clings to my sheets—*her.*

Us.

"I bet you feel like shit."

Mom's voice is closer this time.

So is the scent of the coffee.

I peel one eye open to find her standing at the side of the bed, a mixture of concern and confusion in her gaze. "I...don't feel great..."

She holds out a mug, pursing her lips. "I would imagine not, given how much you apparently drank last night."

How does she...

My head spins, my sluggish brain trying to process what happened to get her here, but I'm clearly still half-drunk. And the half that isn't still lit is *deep* in a wicked hangover already.

I cautiously manage to push myself up onto my elbow and reach a shaking hand up to take the mug from her as my brain thumps against my temples viciously. "Thank you."

She inclines her head slightly and watches me take a tentative sip. I wince at how hot it is, the harsh liquid searing my mouth and my throat, and my stomach twists brutally, not appreciating it, either.

The acidic black coffee doesn't help the nausea situation, but Mom just stares at me expectantly. "Drink *all* of it."

I know that tone, and I am not about to argue with her in my condition. Especially when I have no idea why she's here, let alone how she found out where I was. "Okay..."

Did I call her last night after Ivy left?

Everything is a blur of tears, pain, and really horrific decisions.

Mom retreats from the bed and takes a seat on one of the stools at the counter in front of the other mug she poured, pointedly turning on it so that she's facing the bed and watching me.

I shift up until my back meets the headboard, running my free hand through my hair to keep it off my face. The pounding in my head only increases the more vertical I am. The sledgehammer has now become a fucking jackhammer drilling against my skull relentlessly. "What are you doing here?"

A dark brow rises at me, the reprimand already there without her saying a word. She toys with the mug handle as she keeps her assessing gaze on me, almost as if she's waiting for me to volunteer something. "Ivy called me last night..."

Shit.

I freeze with the mug halfway to my lips, watching her over the rim.

Her eyes narrow on me. "Imagine my surprise when she told me you were in town."

"Yeah, about that—"

She holds up a hand to stop me. "She was hysterical. I

tried to get her to calm down, to tell me what happened, what was wrong..."

Everything is wrong.

Literally everything.

I swallow thickly, really wishing I hadn't taken that sip of coffee, as it now threatens to come back up. "What did she tell you?"

Mom holds my gaze, unwavering, cripplingly intense, the way it always was when I was a child and she knew I had done something wrong but was trying to get me to come clean without having to reveal she already knew the truth. "Not much. Just that you were back, that you were at your studio, and that I needed to get over here as quickly as possible. She said that..." She sucks in a sharp breath, her throat working hard to keep her emotions in check. "That you weren't in a very good place, and she was concerned you might do something stupid if you were left alone."

Fuck.

Ivy wasn't wrong.

I squeeze my eyes closed and pinch the bridge of my nose, trying to breathe in through it and out through my mouth so I don't pass out, or worse, throw up.

The incessant, driving pain in my head doesn't even seem that bad when I consider what might have happened last night if Ivy hadn't appeared.

If she hadn't cared enough, even after everything I told her, to take the heroin from me...

A shiver rolls through me, the acidic bile that now tastes vaguely like coffee climbing my throat again.

I fight it down and force myself to take another sip of

the scalding-hot liquid, as if it might shock my system into some semblance of being able to process. "Is...that all she said?"

Or did she reveal all my secrets?

I don't look up at Mom as I ask it, but I hear her shift, the clank as she picks up the mug and sets it back down on the counter.

"No. She told me to tell you that it's your story to tell, not hers."

Shit...

It would be so much easier if she had just told Mom everything. If the truth were already out there and I didn't have to explain it in excruciating detail to the woman who always loved us and cared for us so deeply, without reservation. No matter what we did. No matter how bad things got. None of it mattered. She was always right there with open arms and a warm hug. Even if she was mad. Or worse, disappointment.

This is going to hurt her more than it does me.

I've been living with the agony and the regret for so long, letting it eat away at me, letting it drive me to do things I knew I'd regret the instant I did them. Everything I fought so hard for could have gone down the drain last night. I was *this close* to throwing it all away.

How do I begin to tell her?

I don't even know what happened after Ivy left.

All I remember is the world spinning, feeling like it was crashing down around me, like everything was coming to an end. Like I couldn't breathe.

And then, darkness.

Mom clears her throat, and I finally lift my head,

opening my eyes to find her brow furrowed deeply above her anguished gaze. "I found you passed out over there." She points to the corner near the windows where Ivy left me. Where I had set up, intent on trying to wash away the pain with the things I had sworn to never touch again. "You smell like you bathed in whiskey last night."

I scrub a hand across my face with a groan. "I did."

The mere *thought* of the taste going down is enough to make me gag.

Mom definitely notices. "I need you to explain what's going on. I need you to tell me why you're here, why you didn't call, and why you look like you just got hit by a damn truck."

It's how I feel, too.

Like Jack Daniels himself drove right over me last night...

And it's only going to get worse.

So much worse.

This isn't going to be an easy conversation, and it's one I've been putting off for far too long. Both because it was too painful for me but also because Mom doesn't deserve any of this. She's better off not knowing what I did and what's happened in the last four years or having to live with the fact that I caused Drew's death.

But last night was a tipping point in more than one.

I slowly nod and throw back the covers, then slide my legs off the side of the mattress and onto the worn wood floor. The movement makes my stomach slosh, and I grit my teeth and gulp back its contents.

Fucking hell...

Squeezing my eyes closed, I inhale a few long breaths, then allow my lids to flutter open and push myself to my feet, stumbling slightly, using my free hand to catch myself against the brick wall.

Definitely not sober yet...

I stumble toward the kitchen with Mom watching every step I take. Her keen gaze tracks over me, taking in what is undoubtedly disheveled hair, a face that hasn't been shaved in days, my bare chest, and the rumpled pants I slept—or more accurately, passed out—in.

Each step hurts as my entire body screams in protest.

But I can't stay in bed anymore.

I can't hide under the covers while she's sitting right here, waiting for an explanation she more than deserves.

The sunlight streaming in from the windows makes me wince, and when I finally reach the island, I intentionally choose a seat that will allow me to settle with my back to the window, facing her, trying to give myself a little reprieve from the pounding in my head however I can.

I set my coffee on the counter and slide onto the stool, releasing a long, heavy exhale filled with all the things I haven't been able to say to her over the last four years.

Some, I still don't want to have to.

Some, I've wanted to so badly that keeping them from her has been as excruciating as my rift with Drew.

Even *one* of the things I have to reveal will break her.

But all of it?

This is going to *destroy* her the same way it did Ivy.

She's already worried. The crinkles around her eyes, the furrow of her brow, and the hard set of her mouth all beg for answers. But nothing I tell her is going to assuage her fears or ease her distress.

Far from it.

I take another sip of my coffee, wincing when it hits my stomach. "There are some things I need to tell you."

Her head bobs slightly. "That's what Ivy said, and given the fact that she was apparently *here* with you, it seems like there are a *lot* of things you haven't told me."

"There are."

I nod.

Where do I even start?

It all spiraled out of control so hard, so fast. And *I* spiraled even harder and faster. Caught up in a hurricane of emotions I didn't know what to do with. Drowning in self-loathing, obsession, and guilt that only made it that much harder to find something solid to cling to.

But ultimately, there's only one place I can start to attempt to explain to this woman why I've lied to her, why I've abandoned her, why I've let myself become someone I don't even want to look at in the mirror anymore because all I see is *him.*

I have to start at the beginning. "Your birthday party four years ago..."

Her brow furrows even deeper, her eyes narrowing. "What about it?"

Rubbing the nape of my neck, I avert my gaze. "I was there."

She jerks back slightly. "You were? I never saw you. I thought you had a show and couldn't—"

I hold out a hand and drop it onto hers, squeezing it tightly, examining how much smaller it is than mine, rather than having to look at her. "I know. That's what I told you and Drew. I wanted it to be a surprise, but"—I release a little mirthless laugh, but all that does is make those knives stab into my temples—"I didn't make it inside."

"Why not?"

Cautiously, I allow my gaze to meet hers again. "Because I met Ivy."

Her eyes widen slightly. "What do you mean you *met* her?"

I clear my throat and pull my hand from hers, instead wrapping it around the mug. And once again, I find myself unable to look at her, instead focusing on the black liquid I'm forcing myself to drink. "She was out in the garden, under the willow, getting some air, I guess." My throat tightens at the memory and how one single decision on my part caused such a catastrophic result for all of us. "She thought I was Drew..."

A moment passes before I hear her sharp inhale.

"Oh, God." Mom's hand comes to rest on my bare shoulder, and I can *feel* her trembling. "Cam, what did you do?"

And there it is...

The accusation in her tone, in her question, because this woman knows me too well, understands how often I let my heart lead instead of my head. How often I leap without looking. How often I fail to see the potential consequences of my actions...

And that's exactly what I did that night.

I leaped, and I fell.

Fucking hard.

For a woman who could never be mine.

I squeeze my eyes closed. "Something that shouldn't have happened."

The details don't matter.

And given the lack of them, Mom certainly knows it went *way* too far.

She makes a little choking noise in the back of her throat. "Drew figured it out..."

I nod, remembering that text he sent me, those five words.

"I know what you did."

Even now, they send a shiver through me. Knowing what they led to, knowing what I caused is enough to make my chest tighten and my body scream for some relief from the pain.

Silence lingers between us for a few moments.

I force my eyes open and look at Mom to gauge her reaction.

She examines me like she's seeing something she never has before.

And she is, in a way.

It's been well over four years since we've seen each other in any way but a video call, and I know she sees how I've changed—not just physically, but the darkness that has clouded me for far too long.

She lifts a hand and rests it on my cheek. "What happened, Cam?"

I shake my head, her hand falling away. "I knew he'd never forgive me, and there was no reason he should, so I went back to London on the first flight out, tried to pretend none of it happened, but..."

"But what?" Her voice wavers, and I can already see her starting to crumble with the reality of what's happened, of what's been hidden from her for so long, of the lie Drew must have been telling her and Ivy.

"I couldn't forget her, Mom." My voice cracks, and I swallow through the emotions clogging my throat. "And I couldn't forget what I'd done to Drew and how I ruined our relationship forever." Staring into my coffee, I remember those days, months, *years,* and all the horrible things I did during them. "I tried to drown myself in anything and everything to deal with the guilt and the... obsession...I had with her." I swallow thickly. "Booze, women"—I meet her gaze—"drugs."

She flinches as if I've slapped her. "No." Her hands tighten into fists on the counter, and she shakes her head. "You didn't..."

I nod, rubbing at the back of my neck where my skin suddenly itches with the memory. "What had been occasional recreational use turned into something else before I even realized it."

Mom's bottom lip trembles as she assesses me. "Your father was an alcoholic..."

My spine stiffens. "*What?*"

She gives me a sad smile. "You two were so young, and he was away training or on deployments so much that I was able to shelter you from the worst of it most of the time. I'm surprised you don't remember something, though."

Memories of my early childhood rush back.

Days spent on the beach with Dad.

Trips to Max's for cheesesteaks.

Playing catch in the yard.

Swimming and splashing.

But a few others push their way to the forefront...

Dad "asleep" on the couch and being unable to wake him.

Mom telling us we had to get out of the house for a while because Dad needed some "alone" time.

And thinking about it now, with the benefit of my own experiences, I know what those mean, and it puts so many events of my childhood into a new light.

"I...I didn't realize anything was wrong back then."

She presses her lips together. "Your dad struggled with what he saw and did during his deployments. He didn't know how to handle it in a healthy way." Her hands twist together in front of her. "He was a good man and a great father, but he had demons, Cam." She chokes back a sob. "I had hoped you and your brother wouldn't go down that same road, but—"

Her head shakes, and she lifts her hand to cover her mouth, unable to finish her statement.

"I had no idea." I run a hand over my face, my temples still throbbing and my mind reeling with this new revelation. "I don't think knowing would have changed anything, Mom. I spent years like that, moving through life like a zombie, looking for any way not to *feel* any of that anymore, but they were all I could think about. And then you told me they had gotten engaged."

Her breath catches, as if she's anticipating where this is going and can already see the crash before it happens.

"And I realized I couldn't let her marry him without knowing..."

"Knowing what?"

I lift my shoulders and let them fall. "Knowing if it would have changed anything if she had known it was me that night. But I also realized what a fucking disaster I was; that I didn't stand a chance at getting her if I went to her the way I was. So, I went to rehab."

She places a hand over her heart, like it hurts badly enough that she physically needs to try to keep it together in her chest. "You were in *rehab*?"

I nod as the tears stream down her cheeks.

"And you never *told* me?"

A sob slips up my throat, remembering how alone I felt, how hard it was to go through all of that without Drew and her or really *anyone* to support me.

I shake my head, the tears threatening to spill from my eyes. "I couldn't because then I would have had to tell you why and..." I swallow back another sob. "I just couldn't. So..." I clear my throat. "When I got out, I knew I had to start wrapping things up in London. I found someone to run the gallery for me, made plans to ship everything back here, but then the invitation came."

Her brow furrows. "What invitation?"

"To the wedding."

Mom blinks rapidly, her eyes wide. "Drew invited you to the wedding after all that?"

"No." I shake my head. "Ivy did. But I didn't know that until last night, when I got this..."

I climb from the counter and walk over to the wall where the box sits on the floor. Mom was probably too worried about me to even give it a second glance when she got here last night.

What would she have thought if she had seen it?

My hand trembles as I reach in and pull out the doll. She sees me approach the counter with it, and more tears well in her eyes. Her hand covers her mouth again.

When she finally lowers it, her lips part on a surprised little huff. "He sent that to you?"

I nod.

She knows exactly what it meant to him, what it means to *me,* what it would have meant if I had received it. It could have changed everything between us.

"He sent it the same day Ivy sent me the invitation, but it didn't get to me. It..." I shake my head, staring at the doll in my hands that suddenly feels like it weighs a thousand pounds, carrying the weight of all my mistakes. "It got lost or stuck in the mail, I guess. But I came back as soon as I got the invitation."

Guilt skates across my skin about how I spent those six months.

Painting and obsessing over her.

Planning my approach and how I would win her from my brother and my best friend.

"I watched them, Mom. For a long time." I look up at her from the doll. "NA tells us to wait at least a year before diving into a relationship, and I knew I was still too unsteady to go to her. But seeing her again? All it did was make my longing even worse. She's like a drug to me. The worst fucking kind because I can't go to rehab for it."

Mom purses her lips, examining me as I struggle to move forward in the story because the next part will tear her apart. "What happened, Cam?" She pulls my free hand into hers and squeezes. "Tell me."

I set the doll on the counter, staring at it as the memories of that night bombard me like a horror movie playing on repeat. "I called and told Drew I was in town, that I was going to tell her everything, that she deserved to know the truth. He showed up here, and we argued." I glance at her, pulling from her hold, unable to accept any form of comfort or affection when the guilt eats me alive. "It was really fucking bad, Mom. And we both said things we shouldn't have, and he left." I swallow the sob that tries to climb up my throat. "He drove off pissed and worried that he was going to lose her to me, and he ran that stop sign and—"

It's her sob that cuts the silence.

And I *finally* let the tears fall.

She drops her head down, burying her face in her hands, and I let her cry.

Because the last thing she wants right now is for me to touch her or to comfort her, not when I'm the reason she lost him.

Each breath I try to take is more of a struggle the longer I watch her.

Her pain permeates the air, makes it heavy, impossible to draw into my lungs fully.

It takes a few agonizing moments before she finally lifts her head and looks at me with tear-stained cheeks and puffy eyes. "Is that why you didn't come to the funeral?"

"I couldn't." I choke on the words. "How could I when I was the reason he was dead? How could I—"

She climbs from her stool and steps up to me, only, instead of slapping me across the face like she would have every right to, she tugs me into her arms, wrapping them around me and holding me like she did when I was a child and skinned my knee.

And I let her.

I cry.

I finally cry the way I've wanted to.

My anguish pours out of me in waves so heavy I soak her shirt, burying my face against her shoulder. Now that she knows everything, it feels like a giant weight has both been lifted from my shoulders and has resettled on my heart because she'll never be able to forgive me.

All of this is my fault.

Every last bit of it.

I don't deserve forgiveness for this from her or Ivy.

And I won't ever ask for it.

I'll take this moment to fall apart, and then I'll let her leave like I'm sure she wants to. But when she finally pulls away, she looks up at me not with hatred, but with so much love in her gaze that it steals my breath.

She swipes at her eyes, then wipes away my tears and takes a step back. "Go shower and get cleaned up."

"What? Why?"

A long, heavy sigh falls from her lips, and she forces a tight smile. "Because I'm taking you to a meeting."

4

CAM

My hand trembles as I flip my one-year medallion between my fingers, the chain that normally hangs it around my neck now dangling below it, tinkling in the quiet room. Holding it used to help settle me. It gave me something physical to remind myself of what I had accomplished. That's why I wore it—to always have it touching my skin and connecting me to something tangible that represented my success.

But today, it feels more like a reminder of my failure.

Because I *did* fail even if I'm technically clean today.

I failed Ivy.

I failed Mom.

I failed Drew.

And I failed myself.

Over and over again, I gave into that part of me that only saw what I wanted, zeroed in on what I *craved*, and ignored the consequences to myself and anyone else.

Envisioning the look on Ivy's face last night confirms I hurt her in the worst way possible. And standing here in front of a room filled with unfamiliar faces—except the one sitting in the back row—all those wrongs I've done to myself somehow seem unimportant compared to the damage I did to *them*.

Mom gives me a reassuring smile, but seeing the tears streaming down her cheeks and her swollen eyes, *knowing* what she's suffering right now, it's impossible to return it.

It's hard enough to stay upright on my shaking legs.

I shove my free hand through my hair, inhale a deep breath, and let it out slowly, gathering myself the best I can to say what I need to today. Because there are so many things *to* say, only the people I really *want* to say them to are gone forever. "Hi, my name is Camden, and I'm an addict."

The chorus of "Hello, Camden" comes back at me, and clutching my medallion in my hand, I rub at my neck.

"I've been clean for 427 days, and I *had* been sober for that long, too...until yesterday." I swallow as the taste of whiskey fills my mouth again, and my stomach churns violently, reminding me of just how much I drank. "And I'd like to say I've been sober for at least today, but frankly, I think I'm probably still a little drunk."

I glance out at the people watching me speak, but none of them look on in judgment.

All I get are sympathetic gazes.

"This isn't my usual meeting, and maybe that's a good thing because none of you know me. And somehow, it seems easier to come here today and tell this to people I *don't* know..."

That's a lie.

It's hard to say this to these strangers, too.

And especially with Mom here.

Because I genuinely never thought I'd be back in this place again.

I thought I had a grip on my addiction and my emotions, but I couldn't have been more wrong.

"I was this close"—I hold my fingers only a few millimeters apart—"to using again last night. I even called one of my old dealers and had him deliver it to my place." A little sardonic laugh slips from my lips. "And it felt like welcoming back an old friend when I opened the door to him. How fucked up is that?"

I shake my head, clasping the small piece of metal like it's a lifeline when last night it was the woman I hurt more than anyone on this planet who kept me from doing something truly stupid.

"The only thing that stopped me from using it when it was *right* there was someone showing up at my place unexpectedly." I flick my gaze to Mom, knowing how hard this will be for her to hear. "If she hadn't shown up, in the next five minutes, that needle would have been in my arm."

And this would have all been for nothing...

My hand tightens around the medallion until the edges dig into my skin.

"I kept telling myself that maybe the alcohol would do it, that maybe once I finished the bottle, I would feel better. That the guilt and agony that were overwhelming me would somehow ebb the more I swallowed. But by the time she walked in, I was three-quarters of the way through it, and all I felt was *worse*."

The pain of seeing Drew's handwriting on that box...

Of opening it and finding the doll...

It rushes back, almost knocking me on my ass the same way it did yesterday.

I had it all so wrong.

From the moment I saw Ivy, I let my addiction to her consume me. And I let it turn me into someone who would believe the worst about the person I loved most in this world...

"I was drowning in it. Stuck in my own head. Suffocated by these feelings that have been building up for the last several months since..." I suck in a sharp breath, trying to swallow a sob that wants to slip out. "Since my twin brother died..."

I squeeze my eyes closed, unable to look at the group or Mom when I say these words that tighten my chest.

"It was my fault. The accident that took his life. None of it would have happened if I'd been in control of myself, if I hadn't been a selfish asshole." Shaking my head, I envision his face as I threw those hateful words at him, as I threatened to take Ivy from him. "I blame so many of the things that I've done on making bad decisions when I was using, but the truth of the matter is, the decision that led me to all this. The one that destroyed my life and so many other people's and took my brother's was one made when I was completely sober."

The garden flashes through my head.

Seeing Ivy on that bench.

The way my footsteps faltered the moment I laid eyes on her.

How my heart stuttered.

How fucking hard I fell in that instant.

I instantly understood everything Drew had been telling me about her over the previous weeks. *Why* he said the moment they met he knew he was going to marry her. I *saw* the way she seemed to just glow in the moonlight, and when she smiled...I was a goner.

But I *knew* it was wrong.

I knew I shouldn't do it, and I did it anyway.

Because I had never *wanted* that way before.

"We always say that we relapse before we pick back up." I rub at that itch on the nape of my neck that won't go away, as if I'm going through withdrawals again. "The truth is, I've been relapsing for years, before I even went to rehab. I just substituted a different kind of addiction. This woman..." I release a little half-laugh that doesn't have any humor in it.

Picturing her face. Hearing those little noises she makes when I'm inside her. Feeling her trembling under my touch and that *rush* that floods my system every time my lips touch hers. "She's intoxicating, and the more time I spent with her, the more I wanted to. The more I *needed* to be around her, to hear her laugh, to see her smile, to know that I put that on her face when she had every reason never to smile again..." I swallow thickly, scanning the room. "Because she was my brother's fiancée."

Several sets of eyes widen slightly at my confession, but Mom doesn't react—either because my confession to her earlier told her everything she needed to know or she was able to read between the lines and saw what had happened before I was even cognizant of it.

"So"—I offer a tight smile, clenching the little piece of metal tighter—"the woman whose life I ruined is the one who saved mine last night." I release a sardonic laugh and shake my head. "And I don't really know what to do with that. But I'm here today, and I still have this." I hold up my medallion. "And I'm going to go back to taking it one day at a time. Or maybe just one minute at a time because that might be all I can handle right now."

A sob threatens to make its way up my throat, but I force it down and look to the back row, to the woman who has every reason *not* to be here after the pain I've caused her. But Mom just offers me a sad smile, her eyes brimming with more tears.

"But I do have a tiny sliver of hope that I might make it through all this...because I have my mom here." I shrug. "Maybe, though I can't see it right now, there's a light at the end of this dark tunnel? Somewhere. I'm not really sure if it does exist—a place where I'm not drowning in the same guilt and agony that sent me down that dangerous road last night. I hope it does, but maybe it doesn't. Maybe I just have to learn to swim harder."

Those dark waves that lapped at the shore when we spread Drew's ashes

Everyone claps, and I step down from the small riser and make my way back toward Mom, unable to look at her as I slide into the chair next to her. I bury my face in my hands, the tears soaking them and my medallion.

She wraps her arm around me and presses a kiss to

the top of my head. "Everything will be okay, Cam. Why don't you come home with me? Come stay at the house."

People start filing past, conversations floating through the air as the meeting concludes, though I didn't even register hearing the final words.

I keep my head dipped low, unable to look at Mom as I decline her offer. "I don't think I can, Mom..."

"You shouldn't be alone right now."

Nodding, I swipe my cheeks and finally lift my face to her. "I know, but...I can't be in that house right now. There are too many memories."

Almost two decades of them jumbled in my head that are hard enough to remember without being in that space, seeing all the reminders of Drew's life that is gone because of me.

It's where we took our first steps together. Where we said our first words. Where we opened Christmas and birthday gifts and grew into adults under Mom's watchful eye and with all her love focused on us so intensely.

I couldn't survive it—walking in that door and those memories flooding me.

Mom presses her lips together tightly. She isn't happy about my refusal, and I'm sure it's a mix of concern and offense that I don't want to be with her, but eventually, she nods. "Okay, but will you please promise me something?"

I want to say *anything*.

But that would be a lie.

There are things I can't promise.

Things I *shouldn't*.

Not when it feels like I'm spinning out of control.

"What?"

Mom holds my gaze, her eyes somehow clear at the moment when I can't seem to stop the tears from falling. "Day or night, anytime, you're going to call me if you need me."

I nod, a sob lodging in my throat. "I'll *always* need you, Mom."

And that's truer than I even realized.

For four years, I've kept my distance, stayed in London rather than coming back here to face the consequences of my actions. I couldn't be in the same room as Drew and not know how badly I wounded him, feel that guilt eating away at me. But that meant hurting this woman as much as it hurt me. Maybe even more. Because she didn't know what kept me away.

It wasn't just what I had done to Drew and Ivy.

It was because I couldn't let her see what I had become.

A shell of myself.

She would have taken one look at me and known I was deep into something I shouldn't be. And that confrontation would have meant admitting my true addiction was to the one woman on the planet I couldn't have.

Those years of excommunicating myself to keep her insulated from my downward spiral tore me apart as much as my guilt and the drugs and alcohol did. Because I love her so damn much and needed her so many times when I couldn't call her, couldn't hop on a plane and fly home to feel her arms around me or hear her comforting words.

But now she knows everything.

All the dark and dirty secrets.

It simultaneously feels like a weight has been lifted off my shoulders and a new one has settled.

Because now that she knows, if I fail, if I take the step that Ivy stopped me from last night, it's going to hurt that much more.

Because I'll be failing not just myself but her as well.

5

CAM

Even the thumping bass that vibrates the old floorboards beneath my bare feet can't ground me tonight the way it usually does. The rhythmic beat typically helps me focus. It gets my head into that zone where all the visions I see inside it can flow out and onto the canvas without any real thought.

Not tonight.

Not when everything is chaos.

My mind. My body. My soul.

The meeting and then a *very* long talk with Dale did little to dispel any of this misery that threatens to consume me, nor the anger at myself for setting all this in motion.

It lives in each breath I take, as does Ivy's scent that somehow still lingers in this space.

Restless energy crackles over my skin.

I pace the studio around a massive blank canvas laid out on the tarps on the floor, just *waiting* for me to do something—where it has remained for *hours* now while I haven't been able to put anything on it.

My fingers twitch, agitated to pick up the brush and get all this emotion *out.*

It's always been my only outlet.

Even as a child with a crayon in my hand, I would draw the world as I saw it and what I was feeling—first in color, then in black, white, and gray after the accident. It was how I dealt with Dad's death, with Mom's illness, with feeling like I wasn't fitting into my own skin the older I got. It has always been my source of *freedom.*

Yet, I can't do it tonight.

Each time I get close to snagging a brush from beside the waiting palette, I retreat to my pacing, because I can't *see* what it's supposed to be the way I should, the way I always could before.

Because it's been *her* for so long that I can't paint anything else.

But I can't paint Ivy now.

Not anymore.

It's always been so easy because I've memorized every second I've spent with her, locked away each minute detail about her hair, her eyes, her lips, her skin, her smile, the way she seems to radiate a pure light and obliterates the darkness always creeping in on me so I can perfectly capture it.

But all that is gone.

All I see now is the devastation on her face as she kneeled in front of me on this floor and absorbed the horrific truth...

All I see is pity and hatred in the eyes that looked at me with so much warmth only a few days ago...

All I see is her *agony* instead of her *life* and beauty.

I don't want to paint her like that.

I don't want to memorialize her pain.

I want to remember her like *that*...

My gaze drifts to the painting I did of her on the bed.

Hooded eyes filled with contentment and a lingering haze of lust gaze back at me with so much affection.

Full breasts and dusky pebbled nipples as my gaze devoured her.

One long leg propped up, exposing her glistening cunt still filled with the evidence of how I took her right in that spot.

"Fuck..."

My scream of frustration echoes around the studio and off the brick and steel the same way her cries did that night and the next morning, but it was so quickly replaced by her sobs of despair in this same space that it's tainted now.

No amount of trying to shake away those visuals or sounds from my head has worked. Ivy's pain is so deeply embedded in my soul that it's become a part of me I can feel with every agonizing breath I take.

That same demon that threatened to control me last night crawls across my back, settling on my shoulders with its agonizing weight. Whispering in my ear that it will help end the suffering and silence the voices in my head. Promising it can ease torture and wipe away the memories...

Only, I know it's a lie.

One I allowed myself to believe for a long time.

One that almost convinced me last night.

One that is so damn tempting when I'm here with darkness and regret as my companions, when nothing seems right and I know that it never will be again.

Too much has happened.

Too many mistakes.

Too many lies.

Too many deeds that can't be undone.

My eyes land on the huge canvas where I made love to Ivy for the first time. Every drop of paint screams in my head. Every splatter makes my chest tighten. Each smear spread across the surface drives a knife straight into my heart.

It represents everything I ever wanted but never deserved. The culmination of me finally succeeding in taking what I always wanted, what I *craved* more than life itself.

And she was *everything* I thought she would be and more.

I start trembling as tears pool in my eyes.

Because it's the most beautiful thing I've ever created, and I'll never be able to look at it again without knowing what it cost me.

It will always be a reminder of all the horrific things I did to get us to that point. I betrayed Drew. Lied to her. Stalked and watched while I lived in a dark hole of selfishness. Threatened and said horrible things I didn't really mean. Then, when I should have left, when I should have let her grieve Drew's loss and found somewhere I could have let myself crumble on my own, I was too selfish not to walk away. I let her need me. I let her kiss me. I let myself give in to all those cravings.

And I'll never have her again.

I'll never touch her, kiss her, hold her, or feel her come apart in my arms.

I'll never get to tell her how sorry I am for everything I've put her through because she will never want to hear it.

Just like I don't want to listen to the sinister voices in my head right now.

I try to shake them clear, squeezing my eyes closed and fisting my hands in my hair hard enough that my knuckles ache and my scalp stings. The pain there doesn't do anything to alleviate that in my chest.

My phone dinging with an incoming message finally forces me to release my death-grip and make way over to the counter where I left it. Hope blooms for a brief moment that it might be Ivy. That she is reaching out to me, that last night wasn't the end...but I know it's likely Mom. And if I don't respond to her, I know she will show up here worried, when that's the last thing I want to cause her ever again.

MOM

Are you okay? I can be there in twenty minutes.

Despite how distressed I am tonight, her offer tugs the corners of my lips up. Because even though she has countless reasons to want nothing to do with me, to hate me, and want to stay far away, she still loves me. Somehow, she has the ability to separate what I've done from that commitment to me and her belief in who I am at my core —a good person. That little boy she raised to always do the right thing and to care about other people more than he did himself.

Even if she's wrong.

At my core, I'm the person who chose himself over and over again. Who did wrong in more ways than anyone can count. *I'm* the one who should be gone from this world, not Drew.

It should have been me.

That truth has haunted me endlessly the past few months.

There were so many times I cheated death, when I came close to the final sleep because of too much booze or mixing volatile concoctions that should have taken me from this world. Yet *he* was taken. The person who literally saved lives for a living, who took care of everyone else, even to his own detriment.

How is any of that fair?

My thumbs hover over the keyboard.

I'm definitely *not* okay.

I'm self-aware enough to know that.

But having her here wouldn't change anything.

Drew will still be gone...

Ivy will still be lost to me...

I'll still know it was all my fault...

Releasing a ragged breath, I fire off my reply.

> I'm fine. Have you spoken to her?

I don't need to tell Mom who "her" is.

As despondent as I have felt since I opened that box, Ivy has it a thousand times worse.

She opened that door for me.

She gave me the key.

She invited me into her home and into her life.

She welcomed me into her heart when I had no business being there.

And I crushed what hope she had left.

I can't even imagine what she must be feeling right now, how bad it has gotten for her...

Bile climbs my throat just thinking about what she's suffering, and I swallow it down, clenching my phone tightly as I wait to hear even a single word about how she's doing.

It took all my willpower and strength not to go over there today to check on her, to ensure she's all right, even though I know she never will be again.

The only thing that held me back was Mom's assurance that she was going to do it and reminder that Ivy would make it very clear if and when she was ready to see me.

Which certainly isn't now.

The little bubbles tell me Mom is typing a reply, but they go on for so long it's clear she is choosing her words carefully. When the message finally pops up on the screen, my hand tightens on my phone.

I went over there earlier. She's understandably upset. Marlo is with her. I'll keep checking on her.

And you.

She didn't have to say the words for me to understand the meaning: Ivy is in as bad a shape as I imagined.

And that demon whispers again...

I block it out, setting my phone back on the counter and turning to face the blank canvas again.

The music continues to play, helping drown out those voices I'm trying so hard to silence tonight, but it won't be enough. So much tension has built through my body that every muscle aches and trembles, and knowing Ivy is suffering only makes it worse.

Instead of grabbing the paintbrush, I snag the box cutter from the counter—the very one I used to open the package from Drew.

I tighten my hand around it, my gaze traveling over the hundreds of paintings in the studio. Piles and piles of them lean against the walls. Almost all of them of Ivy.

But I can't touch them with this blade.

I can't destroy what I have left of Ivy, even if I have destroyed *her*.

My hand flexes around it, though, urged to shred *something*, to make *anything* look how I feel on the inside— flayed alive.

The stereo moves to the next song, and the change in beat propels me forward, those familiar vibrations through the floor comforting as I approach my target.

It's the painting that made me a household name—the one *everyone* recognizes.

They may not know my street art, those murals painted on the sides of buildings in unsuspecting neighborhoods. But they know *this*.

The little girl smiles back at me, holding her balloon

so tightly, the simple joy of receiving it enough to brighten her face and the world around her.

I don't know why this image came to me that day.

I don't understand how it was so crystal clear.

But I *had* to paint it, give it to the world, make a statement about those joys in life we take for granted as we grow up and allow outside forces to crush us.

Now, she seems to mock me.

Because there is no joy left in my life.

I bring the box cutter blade to the canvas and slash it across, ripping through the image and tearing myself open in the process.

Tears stream down my face, but I keep cutting, obliterating it until nothing remains but pieces dangling from the wood and scattered across the floor.

My chest heaves with a sob, and I turn away from it, my vision immediately zeroing in on the blank canvas that has haunted me all night.

I turn the blade on it next.

Slicing.

Stripping the canvas away until nothing remains.

There was nothing there anyway.

There might not ever be again.

My muse is gone, along with any hope of ever finding her.

6

IVY

Man has invented so many brutal ways to torture someone.

Vicious machines and implements that inflict the worst types of pain imaginable.

Each one with the goal of *breaking* the victim—physically and mentally.

These devices wear down a person's resolve. Their ability to handle the torment is stretched to the very limit until it *snaps*. But nothing could possibly compare to *this*.

The agony that wracks me now won't let up. Not even for a second. Not even when I scream and beg. Not when I pray and make deals with a God I'm not sure I believe in.

It's like death by a thousand cuts, only instead of dying and finding relief from the torment, I'm stuck suspended and at its mercy.

And those cuts just keep coming.

From a blade with sharp cheekbones, haunted blue eyes beneath thick, unruly dark hair, and a touch that once brought me back to life when I thought nothing and no one ever could.

It sinks into me.

Flays apart my skin.

Digs deep into my flesh.

Not a thousand times.

Not even a million.

Relentless slices and stabs straight to my chest...

Driving into my heart...

Gouging it and tearing it to shreds...

Until there's nothing left there to beat.

Nothing to keep me going.

7

CAM
ONE WEEK LATER

No matter how many times I've seen this painting, the countless hours I've sat here, staring at it over the years—or looking at it online when I felt the urge to see the brutality and fall into self-reflection from somewhere else in the world—I always manage to find something new that I didn't notice before.

Prometheus's bicep tense and rippling with his pain...

The veins bulging in his forearm as he fights the torture...

How tightly his hand clenches in agony...

The eagle's talon digging impossibly deep into his eye as it tears his liver from his abdomen...

All those little intricacies that make it so gruesome and so beautiful all leap out at me now, and I can't tear my eyes away from it.

It doesn't matter how often I've examined it; it still

captivates me, still draws me in, still makes me question every decision I've ever made in my life.

Especially on a day like today.

When I have to take this step and face one of those *unintended consequences* I've been putting off for far too long.

At least my spiral last week proved a positive step in one regard; it's forced me to do something I should have a long time ago—make amends.

I hurt so many people while I was caught in the throes of my addiction, and I spent so much time focused on getting clean and staying clean for *one* reason that I ignored all the other damage I caused along the way to others.

But not anymore.

Finally revealing the *full* truth to Ivy and Mom ripped open something that I can't hold closed with sheer will any longer. I have to do something to try to stem the bleeding.

Otherwise, I'll be stuck just like Prometheus, in this endless loop of agony.

The click of heels against the museum floor announces Roxy's arrival before she rounds the bench and stops in front of me with a little grin tilting her lips. "I'm glad you called."

I return the smile and motion for her to sit next to me. "I'm sorry it wasn't sooner. Things have been..." I shrug and scrub my hand over my cheek, which is covered with several days' worth of stubble. It's impossible to describe how awful the past week has been. Sleepless nights and tormented days. Indecision and restlessness. The only things that have kept me grounded are Mom, meetings, and the knowledge that it is in my power to face *all* the things I did and do what I can to rectify them. With Ivy, that's impossible, but with Roxy, I can at least *try.* "Things have been a little crazy."

She settles next to me, crossing her long legs, exposing the smooth expanse of skin up to her thigh where the hem of her dress rests at a barely decent level. The delicate heels on her feet scream sexy yet professional, exactly what she has always been. Wicked smart and talented, not to mention stunningly beautiful.

Any man would be lucky to lock it down with her.

But she was never the woman who held my heart, even though I always cared about her as a good friend.

Her gaze rakes over me, taking in every detail of my appearance, which I'm sure is as haggard as I feel. "Good crazy or bad crazy?"

"A little bit of both." Because it *was* good to finally see Mom and get everything off my chest with her. But everything else... "Mostly bad."

Really bad.

Roxy winces, pressing her lips together. "I'm sorry to hear that."

I nod as I lower my elbows onto my knees and rest my face in my palms. "You've got a little bit of time?"

Her eyes dart to her watch, and she nods. "Yeah, I'm on my lunch break, so do you want to go somewhere and grab a bite?"

"I'd rather talk here, if that's all right."

Something about being in front of this painting helps focus me, drowns out that demon settled on my shoulders that whispers in my ear nearly constantly now, despite all my best efforts to silence him.

I look over at her and find her brow furrowed, eyes narrowed on me.

Roxy leans closer. "What's going on with you, Cam? When I saw you here, I told you I'd been worried about you, and it's true. I've been thinking about you a lot since then."

I nod and swallow through the tightness in my throat. "Me, too." Ever since my talk with Ivy and then Mom, I haven't been able to stop thinking about the other people I've hurt, whom I care about. All those who cared about me, too, but who got bulldozed by my addiction—to drugs and Ivy. "I owe you an apology."

Her eyes flare wide. "For what?"

"You know for what." Tension seeps into my shoulders, stiffening them and tightening my neck as the memory of the night we spent together that never should have happened flashes vividly through my mind. "What happened between us, it..." I shake my head, trying to clear away another mistake that had unintended consequences. "It wasn't right. I shouldn't have allowed it to go that far, not when I was so fucked up and I knew how you felt about me."

She presses her lips together firmly, tilting her head slightly as she assesses me. Roxy has always been incredibly observant. Even back in art school, she was constantly analyzing everything and everyone, pointing out flaws in their artwork, not because she was trying to be mean or rude but because she could *see* things others could not.

It's part of the reason we became such good friends.

I trusted her to tell me the truth, even if I didn't like it.

Yet, I never told *her* the truth about what was happening with me when I crossed that line that had been drawn in the sand with her.

Her gaze sweeps over me, as if she's seeking some physical evidence of what I was going through when I made that very unwise decision with her. "How bad was it?"

Shit.

I scrub my hands over my face and sigh. "Bad."

By the time I heard they were engaged, I had fallen so far down the dark hole of addiction that it felt impossible to climb out of it. I scraped and clawed at vertical walls, trying to do just that, ripping my fingertips apart and get nowhere. Only the driving need to see Ivy again and reveal the truth to her, to stake my claim and voice my intent to fight for her, got me through the physical and emotional agony of changing my life.

"I heard you went to rehab not long after."

Nodding, I run my hand through my hair, cracking my neck. "I did."

Because what happened with Roxy was part of that wake-up call.

She was my friend. One of the people closest to me. One of the few who knows I am Cush and who I could ever trust with that secret. Yet I used her as if she were nothing more than a warm body to keep me distracted from what I *really* wanted.

One of her brows rises. "And then you came back home?"

I nod, rubbing at the tension in my neck. "And then I came back home and did even worse things than I did when I was using."

So much worse.

Those years I allowed myself to be sucked into that dark vortex, I made many mistakes and did countless things I regret. But it all pales in comparison to what my selfishness has done to Drew, Ivy, and Mom.

I finally got myself back on track, but that track led in only one direction—toward a woman I never should have wanted or tried to take.

Now we're all suffering because of it.

Roxy winces, wrapping her manicured fingers around the edge of the bench we're sitting on. "Oh. This have anything to do with the girl who was with you when you were here last?"

It has *everything* to do with her.

It always has.

I nod and blow out a long breath. "She was my brother's fiancée."

Roxy's eyes widen, and she whistles, drawing the attention of a few patrons walking by and examining other pieces. Once they've reached a safe distance from us, she leans a bit closer, offering me a sympathetic smile. "All I heard was that he passed away..."

My eyes start to burn, and I clear my throat, trying to dislodge the boulder suddenly sitting there. "Yeah. A car accident."

"Were you and he able to resolve your differences before that?"

This woman wasn't only my confidant when it came to my secret artistic identity. She was there more times than I can count when I just needed to vent to someone. Though I never told her the *whole* story about the rift with Drew, she knew I had done something to drive that wedge between us that he thought was unforgivable.

Or at least, *I* thought he believed that...

Though, now I know how wrong I really was.

The image of the doll sitting in that box flashes before my eyes, and the room starts to blur as tears well.

I was so wrong about everything...

My gaze sweeps up to Prometheus's plight again before moving over to Roxy, who genuinely cares even after I broke her heart by rejecting her after our one night together. I ruined our friendship because I wasn't in control. Because I let my feelings for Ivy and frustration about the situation with Drew get the best of me and turn me into somebody I wasn't before.

It's what prevented me from reaching out to Drew, too.

"We weren't, unfortunately."

Her gaze softens, and she squeezes my hand. "I'm so sorry. I know you two were close for so long. I can't imagine what it must have been like to have lost him when you weren't on good terms. Is there anything I can do?"

I shake my head. "No, but I appreciate the offer. I'm just trying to make things right as much as I can, and it turns out there are far too many unintended consequences for me to do that."

Not in ten thousand lifetimes.

I gaze up at the painting, and out of the corner of my eye, I see her head turn to it, too.

Her lips tilt slightly, but the smile isn't warm. It's hard. Contemplative as she examines it, even though she sees it every day. "*Prometheus Bound.* That's what it's about, isn't it? Unintended consequences?"

I nod, and she tilts her head, cutting her gaze to me.

"Do you know why Zeus chose this punishment for him?"

"Yes." I nod slowly. "I've read the play."

She laughs lightly. "I found it a little boring, to be honest, but *my* understanding is that the liver is regarded by the Greeks as the holder of intelligence, the soul, the heart of life, so to speak. And so, when Zeus set this perpetual torture, Prometheus's regenerating liver every day for the eagle to devour again and again and again, he was striking at the very things that made Prometheus so captivated by man. The intelligence he gave them, the art he gave them that spoke to their souls, the *life* he gave man by allowing them to thrive in beauty." Her eyes lock on me, and even with my focus straight ahead, I shift restlessly under her scrutiny and the topic of conversation. "You know *you* do that, right?"

I turn my head fully toward her, unsure where she's going with this. "What do you mean?"

A sad smile pulls at her lips. "You give people art. You speak to their souls. I've watched you grow since art school, and even though I know better than to reveal your secret, I can't help but want to scream from the rooftops that 'I know him!' Because God, you're so *fucking* talented."

My cheeks heat at the compliment, and I drop my head down. "I didn't come here looking for compliments, Roxy."

"I know that, but it's still true. Your pieces, especially the ones you leave in the most unexpected of places, always have a message people need to see. Something poignant about life, the struggle of man, love, regret. All the things we all feel and sometimes can't express." She releases a little laugh. "You somehow do it with something simple like a little girl holding a balloon. We all remember what *that* felt like as a child. The simple joy of clutching that string in our tiny hand and having the colorful friend floating along with us. It said so much so simply, that we all needed to remember those moments when our struggles made the world seem bleak. That's why people love your work, Cam. And we haven't seen much from you lately..."

I offer her a wry grin. "My recent works aren't really fit for public consumption."

Not when they're all Ivy and have been for years.

Roxy offers me a tight smile. "Well, I hope that changes soon and that you're back to being the Cush we all need and love."

Love?

Did she love me?

I knew she had feelings for me beyond friendship. We had danced around it over the years, flirting and casually joking about hooking up. But neither of us ever took that leap. Until I was already falling and looking for *anything* to cling to.

"I really am sorry about everything."

She leans over and presses a kiss to my cheek. "I'm a big girl, Camden. I knew something was happening with you. I didn't understand the depths of your addiction, or I would have tried to intervene, but I knew that night that you weren't running *to* me but *from* something." Her slender shoulders rise and fall. "I think, deep down, I had hoped things might change between us after that. They didn't, and that's okay. I still value our friendship. And I hope now that we're both here in Philly, things won't be awkward."

I shake my head, my heart swelling at how easily she's willing to forgive me when I don't really deserve it. "They won't."

Because besides Mom, she's the only person I have left in this world I can turn to, and one day, I may come completely clean with her about what went down with Drew and Ivy, though I have a feeling she already suspects as much.

She climbs to her feet. "Good." Facing me, she smiles. "Now, I'm starving. If we've gotten over the whole making-amends portion of my lunch hour, let's go down and at least get a coffee at the café."

I grin at her. "Deal. But I'm buying. I owe you at least that much."

Her light laughter fills the gallery. "Well, in that case, you can buy me something to eat, too."

Pushing to my feet, I can't help but allow my gaze to

fall back onto the painting where the eagle feasts on the source of Prometheus's wisdom and what holds his soul.

For years, it's felt as though I was being picked at, something eating away at me from the inside, but now that I know the truth about how Drew felt and what I caused, it's suddenly become so much worse.

That bird looks harmless compared to the demons tearing me apart.

8

CAM
SEVEN WEEKS LATER

A s I stare at the canvas lying at my feet, Roxy's words from weeks ago continue to ring in my ears, just as they have every time I've picked up a paintbrush since our talk.

"Your pieces, especially the ones you leave in the most unexpected of places, always have a message people need to see. Something poignant about life, the struggle of man, love, regret. All the things we all feel and sometimes can't express."

Before Drew's death, I never had trouble expressing *anything* this way. Whether I was angry, frustrated, happy, confused, high, lonely, or just strung out, I've always been able to vent it through my art. And it's always felt *right* once it's on the canvas or wall.

But now, there are so many things I *can't* express.

Either because I haven't figured out what I'm actually feeling when my emotions are a conflicting jumble or because there isn't any way *to* truly do it.

I've spent countless hours since the night I finally

confessed everything to Ivy trying to figure out a way to tell her how sorry I am without inserting myself back into her life when I know I'm not wanted there. But there are no words that can accomplish that, if she'd even hear them.

The only thing I *can* do is continue sending her favorite meals to the house every day, even if it's woefully inadequate to express everything I feel toward her and this horrible situation I've forced us into, and she's likely throwing them away…

I'll keep doing it until she tells me to stop.

Maybe some part of me is hoping she *will* because then she'd at least be *talking* to me, even if it is to scream and rant and tell me to leave her the fuck alone forever. It would be better than the reality I've been living—or, more accurately, barely surviving—in since she walked out my door that night.

Because this *silence* is deafening.

I hadn't realized how much I've come to rely on having her around and in my life, on being able to ride over to her house and let myself in when I needed to be surrounded by her and Drew, when I needed to see her, to sit and talk, or just listen. And the longer we go without speaking, the harder it becomes to stop myself from going there, not merely to check on her and make sure she hasn't returned to that dark place I found her in—or worse—but to throw myself at her feet and beg for the forgiveness I *know* she can't and won't give me.

How could she?

I still don't understand how Mom sits across from me when we meet for coffee or lunch, knowing I'm the cause of all her pain. Those eyes of hers that I know match Drew's and mine, even if I can't see the color anymore, somehow still hold the same affection they always have, as if everything I've done hasn't changed anything for her. And none of that makes sense to me.

Maybe it's true what people say about having children —that there's literally *nothing* they can do that can change the way you love them.

But that isn't true for Ivy.

The moment she knew the *full* truth, I watched her eyes shutter, and a wall built up around whatever might be left of her heart that will never fall when it comes to me.

I got everything I wanted for a fleeting moment, and even though it was tainted by what I did and lost to get there, it's the only thing keeping me moving forward at the moment. The only thing keeping me sane besides my meetings, my time with Mom, and the fact that at least I'm finally able to put paint on canvas again.

After weeks of nothing, at least I'm expressing *something*.

Only it isn't Ivy anymore.

Every time I've brought out a new canvas since I met with Roxy, a different face has appeared.

One that I look at every day, yet it isn't mine.

Finally revealing the truth to Ivy and Mom somehow turned my guilt into something physical.

I didn't understand why I couldn't paint anything for so long, but after sitting in front of Prometheus that day, it became clear that my subconscious had been trying to get me to put something I didn't *want* to see on the canvas.

That's why I couldn't put paint on canvas or anywhere else. It wasn't just not wanting to see Ivy in her anguish; it was because I didn't want to see *him*.

Drew...

The literal other half of me.

The person who was always at my side and *always* had my back.

The only one who ever really understood me and never tried to change what I was, embracing all my quirks and darkness that clashed so much with the light and warmth that always seemed to radiate from him.

He was my rock.

And instead of telling him that, instead of celebrating his joy at finding Ivy and having her in his life, I tried to take her and destroyed them both in the process.

I will never be able to make up for what I did to Ivy. I will never be able to make things right with her. But at least she's still *here*. And I will spend every minute of every day until I draw my last breath *trying* to find a way.

But he's gone.

There *is* no apologizing to him.

There *is* no opportunity to supplicate myself and beg for him to allow me to take it all back like I had intended to that night after he drove away.

It's too late, and *that's* what I knew but never wanted to face fully until I sat there with Roxy and really *looked* at Prometheus.

It's always been about *him*.

I spent my time so focused on Ivy and her pain, making sure *she* was all right, that I was ignoring the bigger agony that drove me into that bottle and back to my dealer. I was avoiding what had been tearing me apart and going on as if I weren't missing half of myself.

But there was only so long that could continue.

Only so long I could go on with half of my heart.

Now, I'm forcing myself to face it. To face *him*. To face the loss and the guilt and all the decades of life we had together.

Over and over again.

Dozens of paintings over the past several weeks, since my conversation with Roxy finally knocked loose whatever block was preventing me from fully facing the future without him.

Only, it isn't enough.

It's *never* enough.

No matter how many times I paint him, it doesn't feel *right*.

Each brushstroke flows as if I'm possessed. The paint hits the canvases without me even having to think about it. So many memories of him seared into my brain, brought back to life, yet something deep in the center of my chest still stings when I look at them. Another voice in my head screams that they're all wrong.

I stand in front of another one today, paint dripping from the bristles of my brush.

Drew stares back at me from the canvas.

But it isn't the Drew from that night, from the last time I saw him.

So angry.

So hurt.

So broken by what I had done and was threatening to do.

It's the one I *want* to remember, even though it was almost five years ago that he last looked at me this way, that he last held this unrestrained affection for me. Back when he was so excited about his future as he finished up his residency. Ready to find the woman he wanted to spend the rest of his life with and start it. Happy and hopeful about everything that was coming his way.

He grins at me from the canvas, and the words he said before this exact moment in time run through my head. *"It's time you get your shit together, too, Cam."*

If he only knew...

Of course, back then, he meant in terms of settling down with someone, because I mostly *did* have it together. I was focused on my art. Traveling the world and creating beautiful murals wherever I felt like putting them. Expressing all those things that had filled my head before Ivy became my obsession and a devastating addiction...

Before the man I'm looking at now paid the price.

"Fuck..."

The longer I stare at it, see the glimmer in his eye, the crooked tilt of his lips, the more the *wrongness* grows exponentially deep in my chest, expanding until I can't draw in a breath or bear to look at the painting anymore.

Why the fuck doesn't anything feel right?

I throw down the brush, grab the tray of paint, and dump it across the canvas, effectively washing away my work and that memory.

Because it isn't right.

Nothing is.

Maybe nothing ever will be again...

I shove my hands through my hair, tugging at the long

strands that have grown even more unruly in the past several weeks, but no amount of physical pain seems to alleviate the true one I'm feeling.

Something else can...

My body vibrates, and that little voice keeps whispering in my ear...

I shake my head, trying to force away the divisive thoughts that will only lead me down a road I never want to go again.

But it's been a real struggle to silence them.

Meeting after meeting. Talking with Dale. Even the time spent with Mom and some very frank conversations with her about all the things I kept hidden from her for so many years have helped keep me on the straight and narrow.

Barely.

On days like this, the pain and restlessness start to become too much even for the strongest of my resolve.

I have to get the fuck out of here...

If I don't, my eyes will keep drifting to all the paintings along the walls. The ones I destroyed. The ones of *her* I can't bring myself to. The ones of *him* that are all so fucking *wrong.*

Wrong.

Wrong.

Wrong.

FUCKING wrong.

I stalk over to the counter where my cigarettes sit and snag them.

Because what I told Ivy that night was true—I smoke so I don't put worse things into my body.

And today, I want Drew back. I want her. And I want those worse things.

The metal squeals along the track as I tug open the loft door, the sound piercing through the storm of voices in my head—at least momentarily—and I hustle down the staircase and shove out onto the street barefoot and shirtless. But the bite of the fall wind against my exposed skin and the cool pavement on my feet barely register.

My sole focus is getting a cigarette lit and in my mouth before I do something stupid—like pick up my phone and call my dealer again, or worse...Ivy.

I light up and start pacing the jagged, cracked sidewalk as I inhale deeply, drawing the smoke into my lungs and holding it there before I release it in one long, slow stream that quickly disappears into the crisp air.

The nicotine hitting my system doesn't stop my body from trembling.

If anything, it only makes it worse.

"Your brother would tell you to quit."

Ivy's words from that day rush back to me, and I wince, looking down at the cigarette between my unsteady fingers still splattered with black and white paint that's likely in my hair and all over me by now.

Christ, I'm a fucking mess...

This dangerous edge I've been walking seems to keep narrowing, and the longer I go without seeing her, without knowing how she *really* is beyond the placations Mom gives me, the harder it becomes to stay balanced on it.

So, I pace and smoke.

Because it's better than the alternative, than falling.

Anything is.

And some part of me believes that it will come to me eventually—the answer.

Some way to somehow *fix* things that are unfixable.

It may be naïve. It may merely be wishful thinking and hoping for something that will never happen, that *can* never happen, but I have to believe in *something* right now. I need something I can cling to in these dangerous waters I've been struggling to stay afloat in, or I fear slipping under the surface.

I've been swimming harder since the day I came clean to Mom.

Fighting with everything I have.

But it doesn't seem like enough on days like today.

I tip my head back and stare at the gray sky overhead, the clouds slowly passing over me, pushed by the breeze that promises winter coming far too soon.

Drawing more smoke into my lungs, I search for shapes like Drew and I used to as children, but all I see are swirling coils of varying darkness that threaten a chilly rain.

A shiver runs down my spine, and I return my gaze to the neighborhood around my building.

It hasn't changed in the almost ten years I've owned the studio, but just like with *Prometheus Bound*, I always seem to find something new to look at out here.

Old, faded brick walls holding up buildings that have stood here for decades line the street. My fingers itch to paint one, and five years ago, I would have without a second thought.

I would throw paint on it so fast that people would go

to sleep and wake to find the completed piece where there was a bare wall the night before.

But that was before.

Before I betrayed Drew.

Before everything felt so *wrong.*

Back when we were truly brothers, connected by so much more than shared DNA and the same face.

Memories flood my head, my eyes burning with tears that blur my vision as I take another drag from my cigarette.

The answer hits me so hard that I stagger a step.

I know what I have to do...

And I don't know why it took me this long to figure it out.

But my plans are interrupted by my phone dinging with an incoming message in my pocket.

It's probably just Mom or Dale checking in, but I know better than to ignore either of them, so I fish it out and scan the screen quickly.

The words take a moment to register, and when they do, my cigarette falls from my hand to the sidewalk and all the smoke rushes from my lungs...

9

CAM

My heart thunders violently against my ribcage as I take the stairs two at a time, charging up them toward the sixth floor of the medical office building.

The elevator would have taken far too long.

I couldn't have just stood there, waiting for those doors to open, wasting all those precious seconds. I couldn't have walked into it and *stood* there casually in the car as if my world isn't falling apart—*again*—while it glided upward.

Paint still covers my hand that grips my phone, and I check it at each landing I hit to see if Mom has responded to me. But all I see on the screen are our original texts.

Either she hasn't seen the final one or she's ignoring my questions intentionally.

Neither option is one I want to consider, given the contents of her message and what that might mean.

MOM

Come to Doctor Christian's office. Now.
It's important.

What's wrong?

I'm okay. Just please come.

I'm on my way, but please tell me what's
happening.

Are you all right?

Yes. I'll see you soon.

What's happening?

Despite her reassurances, panic seizes my lungs, making each breath harder as I push myself to climb even faster.

It's the last place I ever wanted to set foot again, and just pulling up and parking outside the familiar building was enough to make my chest tighten painfully.

This place holds *that* memory.

Of hearing the word "lump" and knowing Mom might not be okay.

I thought I would never be back here once Mom rang that bell and was officially cancer free. That was over fifteen years ago, yet that same fear and crushing anxiety threaten to suffocate me the higher I climb.

Her cancer might be back...

Why else would she be here?

Why would she need me to come?

Nothing about this situation or the vagueness of her

message gives me any confidence that I shouldn't be considering worst-case scenarios.

And given the state of mind I was in when she texted, it's far too easy to go *there*. Especially when she isn't responding to me.

I swallow the lump in my throat as I reach the top floor and yank open the door with a trembling hand.

Get your shit under control...

The last thing Mom needs is me arriving in a panic if she's already upset about some bad news. And if this were something good, she wouldn't be so fucking cryptic.

My stomach roils at that thought as I race down the corridor toward Doctor Christian's office at the far end, skidding to a stop on the linoleum outside the door with his name on it.

Calm the fuck down.

My heart and lungs don't want to get on board with that idea—both struggling to find a normal pattern. Darkness ekes into the edges of my vision, and I squeeze my eyes closed momentarily, praying to find the strength to face whatever waits for me inside when it already feels like I might collapse from the anticipation of it.

I've never been particularly good at controlling my emotions...

And young kids can be cruel.

Which meant I learned to shut down and keep it in. To only release those feelings on the page or canvas, where I would be safe from ridicule. But since Drew's death, this turbulent tangle of feelings has overwhelmed me so completely that there hasn't been any *hope* of getting myself under any semblance of control.

But I have to.

For Mom.

I take several deep breaths until the shaking in my body seems to abate somewhat before I open my eyes again, pull open the door, and step into the waiting room.

The young woman behind the desk looks up, lips twisting into a welcoming smile before her gaze travels fully over me and shutters slightly at my appearance. "Can I help you, sir?"

Given the way I raced over here after receiving the message, I'm sure my appearance is as much in disarray as my mind is.

"Umm..." I scan the waiting room, but it's empty. With no sign of Mom, I keep working on drawing air into my lungs and releasing it slowly as I approach the desk. "My mother texted asking me to meet her here. Nancy Usher..."

"Oh." Her eyes widen slightly, then dip to the paint covering my hand clutching my phone. "She mentioned you would be coming. Let me take you back."

"Thank you."

My voice comes out far too unsteady and breathless.

Something Mom will certainly notice if I don't get my shit together. Quickly.

Pressing my hand over my thundering heart, I inhale deeply again, clearing my throat to dispel some of the tension so I don't look panicked when I see her.

If her cancer is back, if it's bad news, I need to be the strong one this time.

I need to be the one who keeps it together.

Because Drew isn't here to do it anymore.

He was the one who *truly* stepped up, who took on that caregiver role for her *and* me when seeing her so sick left me in a dark place where all I could see was the possibility of losing her.

If she needs you, you can do it...

That's what I tell myself as the receptionist leads me down a short hallway and pauses in front of an exam room with a closed door. "Here you go."

She knocks once, then opens it wide for me to step in.

As soon as my feet cross the threshold, my eyes immediately go to Mom, who sits in a chair against the wall to my left.

Her gaze connects with mine, shimmering with tears she's barely keeping at bay. She gives me a tight smile, but unease radiates from her. "Thank you for coming."

The receptionist tugs the door closed behind me, but I barely hear it, completely focused on Mom and how swollen her eyes look from crying. My stomach tenses, and I shove my phone into my pocket as I cross over to her.

"Of course." I squat in front of her chair, pulling her hands into mine. "What's wrong?"

Please, God, don't let the cancer be back...

After everything that's happened, I don't think I could survive another blow like that right now—or *ever*.

Mom presses her lips together, locking her gaze with mine. And for the first time in my life, I *can't* read her. She and Drew were always so much alike—wearing their hearts on their sleeves. But now, a strange mixture of emotions swims in her eyes, and even though I can't see their color anymore, I *can* see her uncertainty at the center of them

"I'm *fine*, honey." She squeezes my hands. "This isn't about me."

"What?"

She glances over my shoulder at something behind me, and I turn my head and freeze.

All the air rushes from my lungs, my heart stopping as my eyes meet Ivy's, where she sits reclined on an exam table in a medical gown with a blanket draped across her legs and abdomen.

"Ivy..."

Her name comes out like a prayer.

Because it is one.

Seeing her is like witnessing a goddamn miracle in real life because I never thought I would again.

Only I can't enjoy the moment.

Not when I can tell, even from across the room, that she's been crying, too.

Tears brim her eyes, and streaks trail down her cheeks. Her bottom lip quivers, and her hands twist in the blanket nervously. Something lingers in her gaze that I don't think I've ever seen there before, even after everything we've shared.

Fear.

In all the time I've known her, even over the many years I spent obsessively watching her from across the pond via every single social media post she made or was tagged in, even when she sat a few feet from me and listened to me confess to causing Drew's death, I've never seen *this* look on her face.

Ice-cold terror floods my veins, making my entire body tremble.

Dread settles in my chest.

I drop Mom's hands and move over toward her cautiously, unsure what I'm supposed to do or say as panic tightens around my spine, making each step stiff and awkward.

Why is she here?

Why did Mom ask me to come?

We stare at each other in the silent room, the tension thickening the air the longer no one says anything.

I clear my throat, stopping halfway to her. "What-what's wrong?"

Ivy exchanges a look with Mom behind me, and Mom pushes to her feet.

She stops beside me. "I'm going to let you two talk." Her hand tightens around my arm. "I'll be in the lobby."

Before I can think to ask why she's not staying, she slips out the door, closing it behind her and leaving me alone with the woman who still owns me—body and soul—even if she doesn't want it.

And the fact that she's watching me with that curious look of fear, trepidation, and almost relief twists a knife in my gut.

Fear clogs my throat before I can say anything else, before I can ask anything to try to figure out what the *fuck* is going on.

She gives me a tight smile, clearly uncomfortable with me being here, with whatever she's about to tell me.

That's why Mom left—so Ivy can break the news to me *herself.*

Which means it's bad.

I slowly lower myself into the chair at the side of the exam bed and wait for her to say something, anything, as I hold my breath.

Finally, she releases a long sigh, continuing to twist her fingers in the blanket that covers her lap. "I'm *okay*, Cam. I told Nancy you'd freak out, that you'd probably think she was sick again if she didn't explain why she was asking you to come." Her lips tilt into an almost smile, but it's forced. "And I'm sorry if you did..."

Oh, thank God...

The tiniest bit of tension releases from my shoulders, and I run a trembling hand through my hair, trying to process what's happening. But I can't get my head around any reason Ivy would be here with Mom, or what she could possibly need to tell me when we haven't spoken in months. "It's okay. I, um...now I'm just worried about *you*."

Like I have been since she walked out my door with that almost-empty bottle and the smack that was mere minutes from going into my veins.

Her hands tighten on the blanket, knuckles whitening as if she's having to try to ground herself physically in order to be this close to me. My mind immediately flashes back to how tightly she clung to me like that the night we spread Drew's ashes. How desperately she needed me then.

Things have changed so much.

Now she's nervous. Scared. Uneasy around me when she once craved my touch.

I fucked this up so badly...

She chews on her bottom lip, watching me for a

moment before she releases it. "Really. I'm...okay, Cam, just...a little rattled."

Rattled?

I scan her face, taking in every detail of the woman I've fantasized about for years, searching for any signs of what might be wrong, what might be different. But other than the puffiness around her eyes and the tear stains on her cheeks, she looks okay.

Better than okay.

Fucking beautiful, like she always is.

"Why, Ivy?" I lean closer, my body naturally wanting to be near her even when things are far too complicated for that ever to happen again. "What's going on?"

It takes so long for her to answer that I start to think she won't, but I'm not in any position to be pushing her for *anything*.

Her eyes move from my face up into my hair, then down to my hands. "You were painting..."

I glance down, following her gaze, and stare at the black and white splotches covering my skin. "Um, yeah. Trying to..."

She nods, clearing her throat as her gaze finally sweeps up and meets mine. "Good. That's...good." Her head bobs slightly, and a tear slips down her cheek. "I—"

Whatever she was about to say gets swallowed by her sob, and she presses her hand over her mouth.

A vise tightens around my chest, and I shift closer.

Ivy pulls her shaking hand away, pressing it over her stomach. "I'm pregnant."

My breath catches. "What?"

It echoes in my head.

Pregnant?

The entire world seems to go dark around me, and I blink to clear my vision as I try to focus on her. So much sadness seeps into Ivy's gaze that I can physically feel it like a sledgehammer being driven straight into my heart.

I open and close my mouth, trying to form any coherent thought, but the only thing that keeps playing in my head was her saying *"yes"* when I asked her if I could fuck her without a condom.

Which I did.

Many times.

I assumed her acquiescence meant she was on birth control and there wasn't any chance of this happening because I know her well enough to know she wouldn't have intentionally gotten pregnant when—

"It's Drew's."

Her words cut through the fog of confusion.

"Wh-what?"

Ivy releases a little hiccupped sob, and another tear slips down her cheek, barely contained in eyes locked on mine. "I had no idea. I came in for my annual exam today, and they told me. You know I haven't felt good since Drew died." Her voice wavers. "I couldn't eat because I was always so nauseous and even the thought of most food made me queasy." A sad smile pulls at her lips. "The only reason I ate at all was because you kept making sure I always had my favorite things. I couldn't sleep and was constantly restless and uncomfortable in that bed. I thought it was because he was gone." She releases a little laugh, raising her shoulders and letting them fall. "I thought it was all just...grief. But apparently, it was also because I was pregnant."

"But..."

She reaches under the edge of the blanket and pulls out a slip of paper. Her hand shakes as she passes me the ultrasound photo, and a little zap of electricity rolls through me when her fingers brush mine. "I'm sixteen weeks. Which means I probably got pregnant around the night Drew died."

The world goes black again, and I squeeze my eyes shut as everything starts to spin around me.

Drew's...

It's Drew's *baby...*

Something twists violently in my chest, and if I weren't already sitting, I'd be flat on my ass with the way my body collapses. I cave in on myself as each piece of the agonizing puzzle falls into place, and I force open my eyes again and stare down at the image on the piece of paper and the words typed along the edge in tiny lettering.

Gestation: 16 weeks.

A baby...

Drew's son or daughter...

My gaze drifts over every detail of it—the delicate little hand and fingers already visible. The tiny foot sticking up. The face in profile...

A sob catches in my throat, my hand shaking so badly I'm worried I might not be able to maintain my grip on the photo.

"I didn't even know if I could ever *get* pregnant..."

Her voice cracks, and I swallow thickly and glance up at Ivy.

Tears stream continuously down her cheeks now, her lips trembling along with the rest of her. "I have never had a regular cycle due to cysts on my ovaries. I've had some surgically removed before, and every time they take some off, it causes more scar tissue that can cause fertility issues."

Those tiny scars I saw along her abdomen, that I so meticulously painted as part of *her* flash through my head, the memory of kissing them and exploring every inch of her naked body heating my skin even as my mind continues to spin and try to fully absorb everything she's telling me.

"Drew knew, of course..." She inhales deeply, still twisting the blanket. "We wanted a family. We didn't want to wait until after the wedding to try since we knew it could end up being difficult." Her gaze cuts to mine. "We'd been trying to get pregnant for six months before he died, and it just wasn't happening. We knew it might be impossible, assumed it was after that long, and had kind of resigned ourselves to the fact that we might have to use a surrogate or adopt, but—" More tears trickle down her cheeks, and I have to fight the urge to reach out and wipe them away. She releases another laugh that has no humor in it. "But apparently, I *could* get pregnant the old-fashioned way, just with really, really shitty timing—"

A sob slips from her lips, and it is so filled with anguish that it sucks all the air from the room.

This is all my fault...

It falls one hundred percent on me.

Drew isn't *here* for this.

He isn't here for *her* and their *child*.

He won't see this first photo.

He won't be able to feel his baby kick.

He won't hold Ivy's hand while she gives birth.

He won't snuggle his son or daughter in his arms and know what that kind of love feels like.

He will miss first steps and first words.

He will miss *everything*.

All because I *wanted* what wasn't mine more than I wanted to do what was right.

Agony tears through me, the pain so intense it feels as if I'm being ripped apart. Starting in my chest and spreading outward. Searing. Burning. Stinging. My entire body shakes so badly that I have to grip the arm of the chair with my free hand to keep myself from crumpling to the floor.

Ivy sniffles, unsuccessfully fighting her tears as my own blur my vision of her. "I just...thought you should know..."

"I-I..."

Anything I try to say gets stuck in my throat, and as my gaze drifts from Ivy back to the photo of Drew's baby, I can't breathe.

"Cam?"

I lift my head to meet her worried eyes.

Ivy frowns, her brows furrowing. "I don't want you to think I'm telling you because this changes anything..." Her lips press together firmly, as if she's fighting to stop herself from saying something. "I'm just so *fucking angry*." She sobs, slapping her hand over her mouth as tears flow freely again. "I hate you so damn much for everything you caused, and now this..."

It's too much.

Too much pain.

Too many unintended consequences...

She shakes her head. "So, I don't know why I asked Nancy to get you here. I guess because I don't want this baby to lose his or her uncle when its father is already gone, and the last time I saw you..."

Her words trail off as I force myself to inhale through the crushing weight in my chest.

The last time she saw me, I was a fucking wreck.

Completely unable to cope with the guilt and shame that overwhelmed me.

And truth be told, I'm not much better today than I was that night.

But now that Ivy has seen me like that, that's all she'll *ever* see.

She won't see the man who has held her and made love to her. She won't see the man she said helped her survive during those weeks we spent together mourning Drew. She won't see anything but the addict who was ready to shove a needle into his vein to make it all stop... and who killed the man she loved, the father of her child.

Ivy reaches out and takes the ultrasound photo from me. "You seemed ready to jump off a cliff with no parachute, and I thought...maybe this"—she trails her fingers across the image—"would be your reason never to try that again. Maybe knowing you have a niece or nephew coming will be your parachute if you ever feel like you're falling again."

A tear slips from my eye, leaving a hot trail down my

cheek. I reach up and wipe it away, my heart shattering at the intensity of her words and the emotion behind them.

Because she still *cares.*

Even after *everything* that's happened, *everything* I've done, she still doesn't want me to do something I can't take back, despite her having every right to.

"Does this mean..." I swallow the hope that starts to swell inside me, because I'm pretty sure I know what her answer's going to be. "Does this mean you're going to let me be in this baby's life?"

Because God knows I won't be part of hers otherwise.

And selfishly, I want that, too.

I want *her*, too.

Any way I can have her.

She glances down at her stomach, resting her hands over it protectively, like she already needs to defend her unborn child against the chaos I've brought to her life and the misery I've caused. "I don't know, Cam. I just...knew I needed to tell you." Her eyes clench closed, and she releases a shaky breath. "I can't think about that right now, can't think about anything. I'm still just trying to process all of this without completely losing my grip."

Her voice cracks, and with it, so does my ability to keep my emotions in check.

I push up from my chair, shoving my hands through my hair and scanning over her, taking in every detail in case I never see her again.

There's so much more I want to say. So many things I can't put into words as I stare down at her and the ultimate result of my actions still clutched in her hand.

The night I caused Drew's death, they finally got everything they ever wanted...

Their miracle...

And he's not going to be here to see it.

The only thing that keeps me upright and prevents me from crumpling to the floor is not wanting Ivy to see me like that. Not wanting her to know the depths of my grief and guilt or how completely unsteady I am. Not wanting her to see me so unhinged that she continues to worry about *me*.

She's already seen where it's driven me and how bad it can get...

I swallow through another sob, finally forcing myself to say *something*. "I'm...really happy for you...that you have this piece of him."

And I truly mean it.

Ivy deserves all the happiness in the world.

And maybe...

Somehow...

This baby is the miracle meant to bring that to her.

Before my voice can crack and give away how close I am to completely losing it, I turn and stalk from the room, tugging the door closed behind me without looking back at her. Because if I did, I wouldn't be able to walk away.

I drop my head against the door, squeezing my eyes closed as I take several deep, long breaths in the hallway.

"I hate you so damn much for everything you've caused..."

Her words repeat in my head.

Over and over and over.

But I can't blame her for throwing that at me.

Not now that the true cost is right there in black and white on that ultrasound photo.

10

IVY

I don't know how long I've sat here, staring at the avocado on the counter or the note next to it.

Minutes.

Hours.

It definitely feels like it's been closer to *hours*.

Or maybe I've just been in some sort of alternative reality where time doesn't exist.

That's certainly how it has felt since Doctor Christian told me about the baby yesterday...

And since I saw *him*.

Like I'm existing in some strange alternate reality where what's up is down, what's left is right, and where something that was supposed to be impossible is suddenly happening.

My hand settles over my stomach, but my focus stays on the green fruit and the words written across two Post-its beside it in Cam's handwriting.

The baby is the size of an avocado at 16 weeks.
They're good for fetal development and contain
healthy fats. There's a bag of them in the fridge.
(Along with something else for dinner.)

Tears blur his message, but I don't have to see it to feel its weight.

Cam left that doctor's office and looked this up...

I told him I hated him.

And he went and did *that.*

Then came and did *this* while I was at work today.

Why does that make me *feel like the bad guy when all this anguish happened because of him?*

11

CAM
ONE MONTH LATER

A cool fall breeze whips around me, and I tighten my jacket around myself against the blustery chill that somehow still seeps into my skin.

The weather seems fitting for my mood today.

Dark.

Overcast.

Almost as if the world itself somehow feels exactly what I do and has joined in solidarity with my mood.

The beach is almost completely deserted, the dropping temperatures and promise of an early snow keeping most people away.

Save for the lone figure standing on the sand near the shoreline, back to me.

But I don't need to see her face to know who it is.

I'd know Ivy anywhere.

Anytime.

Anyplace.

My heart calls out for hers, even if she continues to hate me.

Her dark hair floats loose in the frigid wind, but she doesn't seem to notice it, just stands there, staring out at the water that appears even darker today due to the heavy cloud cover overhead.

I glance at my car, tempted to go back to it rather than disturb her when I'm confident I'm the last person she wants to see—today of all days.

The weeks since I saw her last have done nothing to abate any of the guilt eating me alive, nor do I imagine it has any of her anger toward me for how I've ripped apart her life.

"I hate you so damn much for everything you caused..."

Every day, I hear those words and see that ultrasound picture. I watch those tears track down her cheeks and know it's all because of me. Countless hours pass by as I imagine what their baby is going to look like—her soft eyes and Drew's quick, bright smile.

And I'll likely never see my niece or nephew.

At least, not in person.

Mom will show me pictures, try to make me feel connected, but I can't expect Ivy to ever be okay with having me in her life again in any meaningful way.

Yet, I can't walk away from her.

Not today.

Her beauty, her anguish, even her damn anger act like a fucking magnet, dragging me toward her, making my hands itch to tug her into my arms and hold her impossibly close until all her pain melts away.

It's impossible.

But I still move toward her like the obsessed man I've always been when it comes to her.

My boots sink into the sand as I leave the boardwalk and make my way across the beach toward the only person on this planet who can destroy me with a single glance or word.

Each step ratchets up the tension in my body, locking my spine and making my shoulders and neck ache. Weeks of wanting to see her, of forcing myself to stay away and only drop by the house when I was sure she would be gone, have left me starving for her.

A real, painful ache, deep in my soul, that has only grown as the days pass slowly and the nights are agonizingly long and lonely. Filled with endless wondering and worrying about her and the baby...

And now she's here.

Right in front of me.

Looking so fucking beautiful.

She stands, staring at the water with her arms wrapped around her, the collar of her peacoat flipped up against the wind. Her dark hair floats on the breeze, whipping to the side under a particularly large gust, and she shivers.

Fucking hell...

All I want to do is step up behind her and tug her to me, give her my warmth and comfort her on a day that has to be as excruciating for her as it is for me, but I can't.

And that crushing reality lodges something squarely in my throat.

I don't know if she senses my approach, but it definitely seems like her back stiffens as I step up next to her.

She doesn't turn to look at me, doesn't say anything, just keeps her gaze locked on the churning water and the waves lapping at the shore.

"I should have known you'd be here..."

My words sound hollow, as empty as I've felt for the last several months since Drew died, and even more so since the ugly truth came out and Ivy really *saw* me.

Keeping her eyes on the last place we saw Drew, she nods, burrowing herself further into her coat collar.

"I can go, if you want me to..."

I never knew silence could be so loud until this moment, when all I want is to hear her voice again, to hear one single word from her. For her tell me to *stay*.

The longer it drags on with only the sounds of the ocean filling the tremendous distance between us now, even though we stand so close that our arms are almost touching, the more confident I am that she will ask me to leave.

She certainly has every right to.

Especially today...

But when she finally speaks, still refusing to look at me, there isn't any malice in her tone. Only sadness. "It's okay. You deserve to be here as much as I do."

The way her voice cracks makes that lump in my throat swell, and I swallow thickly, trying to break through it before I go and say or do something stupid.

Ivy inhales deeply, her chest rising under her thick coat, then lets it out slowly, arms still wrapped tightly around herself. Her eyes finally drift over to me, and they don't hold any apparent anger. "Happy birthday."

I wince at the words.

Not because I don't think she genuinely means them but because nothing will ever be happy about this day again.

My chest tightens, squeezing my heart painfully as I remember all those years of birthday parties I shared with Drew. Three decades of joy and love that I destroyed so completely. "Thank you, but it's hard to think of this day ever being happy."

Not when it's the first one without Drew. The first one living with the guilt of what I've caused, bearing the weight of what I've cost all of us...

The breeze picks up, the icy chill making me shiver. Ivy does, too, shifting in her riding boots and rubbing her hands over her covered arms.

I can't help but let my gaze drift down to her belly.

With the oversized coat on, it's hard to see the swell, but I know it's there.

It has to be by now.

Drew's child—my niece or nephew—growing inside of her.

And who will never know their father.

Tears burn my eyes, and I blink them away, trying to clear the emotion from my throat yet again, and at the same time, I struggle to figure out what to say.

What can I?

There are no words that won't sound completely hollow at this point.

There is nothing that can be said that will ease any of her pain or my own.

So, I stand, staring at the waves, remembering the last time we were here together to say goodbye to Drew...

And what it led to.

My body heats at the memories of her mouth on mine, of my hands roaming over her body, of my cock sinking into her blissful heat. All the things that haunt my days and keep me awake at night before my guilt douses the fire with icy reality as cold as the weather today.

There are so many things I want to say, things that *need* to be said.

I never got the chance to apologize to her.

She stormed out of the studio before I had an opportunity to say what I wanted to, but she had every right not to want to hear it. Not when I was unraveling like that. Not when I revealed the god-awful truth to her while I was sitting next to a damn needle and bag of heroin.

But this isn't the place or time, either.

Ivy doesn't need my apology, nor does she want it.

What she needs is happiness, something to make her smile, to help her get through the minutes and hours and days and weeks.

Hopefully, that baby will be that thing that pulls her out of this, a reason to keep pushing on when things feel far too hard and far too complicated to do so.

I shove my hands into my pockets, trying to keep them from trembling. But it doesn't have anything to do with the cool temperature; it's more about the cool, icy look in her eyes that used to be so warm when they met mine.

The silence becomes too much, though.

And the longer I look at the water, the more vividly decades of memories race back, and despite how shitty I feel, my chest warms. "We spent most of our birthdays here with our grandmother, on the beach."

"Even when it was this cold?"

A sad smile pulls at my lips, and I nod. "We wouldn't go in the water, just walk on the sand, looking for seashells and cool rocks and any other beach junk we could collect."

Ivy offers me a smile that matches the pain in my heart. "How old were you when she died?"

I tilt my head slightly, trying to remember exactly. "Ten. It was kind of like losing a second mother..."

She nods and returns her focus to the water. "That's how my nonni was, too. It was always just the three of us."

For all the intensely intimate details I know about this woman, there are so many other things I'm still so clueless about.

What the fuck does that say about me?

"What about your mom's father?"

Her shoulders rise and fall. "I don't know if Nonni even knew who he was, to be honest." She releases a little sardonic laugh. "She was a true hippie. Went to Woodstock and everything. Believed in free love. Back then... they were less careful."

I cringe at the implication. "And your father?"

She glances over at me. "Mom never wanted him involved. As far as she was concerned, he was a sperm donor and nothing more, but I never felt like I was missing out on anything."

Images of my childhood flash through my head.

Of birthdays and Christmases.

Hugs and tears.

The man who somehow shaped us, despite not being in our lives for very long...

"Our dad was around...but not much." We were lucky if we saw him for a three-day weekend once a month and then a few weeks here and there while he was on leave. And now, all those memories are tainted by what Mom revealed about Dad's struggles that so closely mirror my own. "I found out he was an alcoholic."

Her head whips toward me, her eyes wide. "Really?"

I nod. "Mom told me that night."

Ivy pulls her lip under her teeth, and guilt clouds her eyes at the mere mention of the night that changed everything between us.

"You did the right thing, Ivy, calling her, getting her over there."

Moisture pools in her eyes, and I don't dare hope that they're for me rather than just caused by the wind and sand. But a little hiccupped sob slips from her lips. "I shouldn't have left you like that..."

She shakes her head, and a tear trickles from her eye before she looks back to the water.

I so badly want to reach out and wipe it away, but I don't have the right to touch her anymore.

No.

I *never* had the right to touch her.

That's what started this whole mess in the first place.

"You needed to get out of there, Ivy. I understand that." I attempt to keep my voice level, trying to stop myself from breaking before I say what she desperately needs to hear. "It was a shitty position to put you in. But you saved my life that night." I release a long, heavy breath, wishing I didn't have to admit this to her. "If you hadn't come over, I..." I squeeze my eyes closed, remembering the vicious spiral I was in, but then I force my eyes open, force myself to look at her and see her agony. "Ivy, please look at me."

She turns her head, and her watery gaze locks with mine.

"It's *okay*. You did the *right* thing." I press my hands to my chest. "I'm the one who fucked up. Over and over again. Please don't feel guilty about leaving because you *had* to."

Her lip trembles, and she nods, twisting back to face the waves. "He wanted to have his ashes spread because he didn't want me to be staring at an urn constantly, but" —she shrugs—"here I am, staring out at the water as if he's still here."

Fuck.

There is no hope of restraining my own tears anymore.

They fall easily, sliding hot down my cheeks and cooling before they drop from my jaw. "He is still here. I feel him every time I'm on this beach."

Which I've been coming to far too much lately.

At least once a week, sometimes more, I stand right in this spot, needing to be close to him even if he wouldn't want this.

"Yeah." Her voice cracks as she nods. "Me, too."

This time, the silence that settles over us is comfortable.

There are so many more things to say, but today is about Drew.

My guilt can wait...

All that exists in this moment is the two of us loving Drew, the lapping of the waves, and the breeze blowing around us.

The temperature seems to drop again, and Ivy shivers more violently.

Immediately, the desire to get her somewhere safe and warm overtakes me. "Should you be out here?"

Her hard eyes flick to mine. "I'm pregnant, not sick."

"I know, I'm just...I worry about you."

Every second of every day, I worry about her and the baby.

And I always will.

Her jaw sets, and her lips press into a firm line. "Well, stop. You don't have to." She shakes her head as if to enforce her statement. "I don't want you to. I don't want *any*thing from you, Cam. Not ever again."

She turns and stalks through the sand back toward the boardwalk, leaving me standing at the waterline alone.

The smell of the ocean, the sand, and all my regrets fills my lungs, and I squeeze my burning eyes closed as I process what she just said.

So much hurt and anger laced her words and voice.

Not that I didn't know that's how she felt, but hearing it from her lips makes it a thousand times worse.

It makes it more real.

It makes any hope I might have had of being involved in that baby's life evaporate in an instant.

Ivy doesn't want me in her life.

She doesn't want me in the baby's.

And that's probably for the best.

But I can't just walk away.

I open my eyes, and tears flow down my cheeks. "Happy birthday, brother. I'll make sure she's okay. I promise."

12

IVY

The bunch of bananas sits in the center of the counter.

Something so innocuous that probably half the homes in America also have waiting to be consumed stirs up a maelstrom of feelings the moment my eyes land on them.

It's far from meaningless in my house.

Tears I would love to blame on hormones rather than conflicting emotions well almost instantly, just as they have every week when the new fruit or vegetable shows up in my kitchen with Cam's notes.

And these...he must have brought them before he came to the shore, after I had already left to drive out there.

My stomach twists as violently as my heart does as I approach them and set my purse on the counter beside the note.

The baby is the size of a banana at 20 weeks.
These are also really good for both of you.

I told Cam not to worry about us, that I didn't want anything from him, and I meant it.

I *don't*.

I *can't* want or need *anything* from Camden Usher ever again.

All wanting him has ever done is destroy my life.

From the first damn moment I saw him in his mother's garden, all he's brought is lies, pain, and turmoil.

I tried so hard to set aside my anger today, to concentrate on why I was standing there in the sand and accept that Cam was beside me for the same reason—that despite everything, he loved Drew.

But my anger has become a living and breathing thing that survives on my grief and feeds off it, staying alive and rearing its ugly head when it shouldn't.

Cam didn't deserve that today.

Not really.

Yet some part of me refuses to let go of any of the pain.

If I do, I'll be letting go of Drew, too.

And I can't ever do that.

I rest my hand over my growing belly where a tiny foot presses against it, and a smile pulls at my lips before the anguish and tears quickly return.

Drew will never feel this...

There won't be any birthdays.

He won't witness his child coming into this world.

And that's why I can't forgive Cam.

That's why I can't let him get back under my skin or into my heart.

13

CAM

ONE WEEK LATER

I t looks so different tonight.

His house.

Hers now.

Darker...

I look up at the porch light I replaced that should be glowing brightly this time of night, but it's off—either because Ivy forgot to turn it on or chose to keep herself in the darkness intentionally.

Probably the latter.

Ever since the beach, I've been worried about her, even more than I had been before that day.

And not just because of how we left things. She had every right to feel that way and say those words to me.

She seemed so...lost.

Alone.

Drifting and hopeless.

So completely devastated in a way that seemed even

worse than how I found her that first night after she'd received Drew's ashes.

I hadn't thought it could get harder than it was at that moment when her eyes met mine through the driving rain and she said his name...

Having to watch confusion and then hope flicker across her face for that split-second before she crumpled into my arms....

But I was so fucking wrong.

About everything.

And there were so many things I wished I'd said as she walked away from me on the beach, but I knew none of them would change anything for her—or *me*.

All saying them would have done is make me seem desperate.

Because I am.

I'm desperate to go back to that night four years ago and do it all over again so fucking differently. I'm desperate to go back to that night months ago and change everything I said to Drew. Instead of threatening to reveal the truth to Ivy, I would congratulate him and drop to my knees to beg his forgiveness. I'm desperate to take Ivy's pain away...

As if that's even possible.

There have been so many things I've deluded myself about, but that isn't one of them.

But it doesn't mean I won't do *anything* I can to make it better for her.

Even if it means facing the same anger she threw at me on that beach, which might very well happen tonight.

I've walked through this front door so many times over

the last few months—uninvited, then welcomed as a friend, as a lover, then uninvited again...yet she hasn't asked me to stop.

It would be easy for her to ask Mom to tell me to stop, or even to reach out herself and demand I stop intruding into her home and her life. To stop with the meals and the notes about the baby. To stop coming in when I know she's gone, like a thief in the night trying to get away with something he knows he shouldn't be doing. But she hasn't.

And that's the only thing that gives me any glimmer of hope where Ivy is concerned.

When everything else, including her own words, warns me to stay away, I keep coming back, moving toward that dim light at the end of the vast dark tunnel, hoping that one day, I might finally step into it and be able to embrace something besides this anguish we both seem to be lost in.

And that's what worries me most tonight—that she's lost somewhere *no one* can reach her and doesn't *want* to be found.

Because she should be at the shop right now.

She should be busy with Marlo and Trina working on the flowers for the wedding tomorrow.

She should be surrounded by people who love her and support her.

But she chose to come here.

To this dark house.

Alone.

Just like she chose to go to the shore alone rather than

asking Marlo or Mom to go with her on a day she knew would be incredibly difficult.

There's a difference between needing space and wanting some time alone to process things and locking yourself away to wallow and waste away.

And I can't allow the latter to happen to Ivy.

I promised Drew I would take care of her and the baby, and that is one promise I will never break, even if it breaks me.

Balancing what I brought for her in my left arm, I pull out the key and slip it in, then unlock the door. I hesitate for a moment before pushing it open. That hint of reservation about whether I should be intruding when she made it very clear she doesn't want me to is enough to make me reconsider what I'm about to do.

But I've never been good at self-preservation or doing things that are in my own best interest.

That's always been my downfall and what has led to just about every shitty decision I've ever made.

Which is why I open the door and enter the home Ivy shared with Drew for the first time in months when Ivy is also here.

Her scent overwhelms me immediately, like blossoming flowers in the spring, despite the fact that nothing truly feels alive in this house. The darkness envelops me, everything still and quiet. I inhale deeply, drawing what I can of her into my lungs since there's a very good chance she is going to kick me out as soon as she realizes I'm here.

I tighten my grip on the items in my left hand and tucked into my elbow before I close the door behind me. Silence lingers as I make my way to the kitchen and place the bag with her dinner into the fridge. I pause for a moment, waiting and listening, but there still isn't any sign of where she might be.

Unease settles in my stomach, and I take the other item I brought for her and set it on the small end table beside the couch next to the photo of her with Drew at the shore the day he proposed.

A place so filled with happy and beautiful memories for us that he made *their* place, only for it to become somewhere filled with the sadness I saw on Ivy's face the other day.

Scrubbing my hands over my face, I take a deep breath and force myself to look away from it before a tidal wave of emotions can overwhelm me.

Fuck.

I've tried so hard to find a way to sort through all these feelings over the past few months, but each time it seems like I might be getting a grip on the constant internal turmoil, that I might be finding a way to make it through a single day without breaking down and having to fight for my sanity and sobriety with every fucking fiber of my being, something sets me back again.

A memory.

A smell.

A single look from the woman whose house I've just let myself into.

She'll hate me for being here, for me having to be the bad guy by not letting her slide down this slippery slope that leads nowhere good.

But I already am anyway.

Always will be.

And I have to keep my promise to Drew and give myself some peace of mind that she's all right.

I make my way past the closed office door and to her bedroom, pausing just inside the jamb, refusing to invade this space that belonged to *them*.

I've crossed so many lines that never should have been, but this one seems more like a vast canyon I refuse to leap over.

Ivy lies with her back to me, her dark hair spread out behind her on the pillow. If she's sleeping, I don't want to wake her, but I need to know that she and the baby are okay.

"Ivy?"

She flinches, as if hearing me say her name is somehow painful to her now, when she used to shiver in anticipation when I whispered it before. I squeeze my eyes closed and drop my forehead against the doorjamb, sucking in a long, slow breath, gathering the strength I need to face whatever wrath she might throw at me tonight.

"What are you doing here?"

Her voice is somehow soft but heavy with a thousand different emotions I've also struggled with so intensely.

I lift my head and gaze at her again—the slope of her exposed shoulder blade, the way her hand rests protectively on her growing stomach, the elegant length of her neck, and the smooth line of her jaw. My hands itch to touch her, to run over her soft skin and absorb all that addictive energy she always puts out.

Instead, I fist them at my sides, preventing me from overstepping—again. "I stopped by the shop to bring you dinner because you usually work late on Friday nights before a wedding..."

She tilts her head slightly toward me, still not looking over her shoulder but clearly listening.

"Marlo told me you left early because you were tired." I swallow thickly. "I was worried."

That probably wasn't the right thing to say.

It was only a week ago that we stood on that beach and she told me she didn't *want* me to worry about her.

And I don't have the right.

Ivy isn't mine.

She never has been.

Even when she was in my arms and my cock was buried deep inside her, she was always Drew's, and no matter how badly I want to believe that could ever change, it won't.

Her heart will *always* belong to him.

And that's how it *should* be.

But even knowing that, I can't just walk away.

I never could when it came to Ivy.

She finally turns her head all the way and glances over her shoulder at me, and teary eyes slam into me so hard that I practically stagger back.

God, I fucking miss her.

Every single part of my soul screams out to close the distance between us, to pull her into my arms and tell her how much I love her and how sorry I am. But she doesn't want that. Doesn't want more apologies that won't change anything. More words that can't undo all the damage I've already caused.

She wants the life she was supposed to have.

She wants the life Drew promised her and would have delivered.

Ivy shifts slightly, returning her head to the pillow and her focus to the wall in front of her. "I'm just tired."

I don't believe that.

Not even a little bit.

She takes her job too seriously and cares about the business and her customers too much to leave early when there's work to do for something as important as someone else's special day...unless she truly couldn't be there any longer.

"Really, Cam. I'm fine—"

Her voice breaks before she can finish, and a sob slips out.

She slaps her hand over her mouth to try to cover it, but it's too late. That heartrending sound slams into my chest so hard that I close the three steps between me and the bed before I can even think about what I'm doing.

I drop to my knees beside the bed and reach out, resting my hand on her shoulder. The smoothness of her skin under my calloused palms makes me shiver, and the heat that seeps from her and through me warms every part that has felt so fucking cold and dead since she walked away from me that night.

Don't.

I can't let myself fall under this spell again.

I can't let myself *want*.

"Ivy, you're not okay..."

Her body trembles as she sobs again, turning her head further into the pillow and away from me.

Shit.

I'm making things worse by being here, and while I'm relieved that she isn't ill and that the baby's okay, this constant agony she's suffering because of me isn't healthy for her or the child she's growing inside her.

I squeeze her shoulder and push to my feet. "I'll go..."

Her hand slides over my hand and catches it before I can pull away. Trembling fingers curl tightly with mine. "Please, don't leave me, Cam."

If I ever had any hope of getting out of here with a single piece of my heart intact, it evaporates with the power of her words and the pure desperation in her voice.

This woman despises me and what I've done to her, but she can't do *this* alone.

At least, not tonight.

Ivy tilts her head back toward me, her tear-soaked eyes meeting mine. "Please stay..."

Whatever else she might want to say is swallowed by another sob, and she clings to my hand as if she's terrified of what might happen if I pull it away, while I'm terrified of what will happen if I don't.

It will be something she'll regret.

I somehow know that with every fiber of my being, but I still toe off my boots and slide into bed behind her.

The bed she shared with Drew.

The bed I *swore* I'd never get in.

But there are so many things I swore I'd never do, so many lines I never thought I'd cross or roads I never believed I would walk, let alone *sprint* down them headlong without any way of ever going back.

And this one is so warm and inviting.

Ivy pulls my hand down around her, urging me closer,

and I shift until my chest presses against her back, her entire body molded to mine so perfectly. She snuggles deeper as my palm settles on the swell of her stomach over hers.

I link our fingers together and bury my face in her hair, inhaling her scent, dragging it into my lungs the way I do the smoke from my cigarettes because I need it just as badly.

Am *addicted* to it.

To *her*.

And these months apart have left me teetering on the edge of a catastrophic fall back into the person I swore I would never become again.

Because she's everything sweet and light and good, while everything else about me and my life is so dark and bad and *wrong*.

I don't know if I'll ever have this chance again...

To be here for her in her moment of need, to give her *this* when I've taken so much from her.

Sobs rack her body as she trembles against me, giving herself over completely to the emotions she has tried to bottle up and keep hidden from Marlo, Trina, Mom, and me...

She wanted me to walk out of here without seeing her like this.

She wanted me to believe she was okay.

But she's so far from it.

I hold her tightly, slipping my other hand under her and across her chest so I can feel her heart beating under my palm and her ribs heaving with each anguished sound she releases.

My eyes burn, and I squeeze them closed, pressing a kiss to the back of her head. "I'm so sorry, Ivy. It's all my fault." The apology I've been choking on and holding back since that night she found me in the studio flows out uncontrolled now in a tidal wave of overwhelming emotions I can no longer contain. "Drew should be here with you right now, holding you like this, helping you through this pregnancy. You should be planning your life together, the nursery, shopping for all the baby clothes and toys, picking names, and I'm the reason he's not here." I swallow a sob, trying to push myself to say what I might never be able to again. "But it doesn't mean you're alone. Please don't ever think that."

Ivy heaves out another anguished sound and shakes her head. "But I *am*. I don't know how to do this, Cam. I don't know how to do it without him."

I tighten my grip on her until her trembling makes my body start to shake, too. Until it feels like my strong grip is the only thing holding either of us together anymore. "You're the strongest person I know, Ivy. Look at what you've already survived. And now, you have this." I press my palm firmly against the swell of her belly. "You have this gift from Drew. A son or a daughter who's going to have all the best parts of him, all those qualities I lack that he had, all those things you loved about him, and every time you look at him or her—"

"Her."

"What?"

She glances back at me, the corner of her lips twitching slightly. "It's a girl. I found out last week."

My brain short-circuits for a moment.

Everything goes blinding white, then onyx black, before the room around me starts to return.

Drew is going to have a daughter...

I'm going to have a niece...

Who's going to grow up without her father.

Images of Drew chasing a little dark-haired girl down the beach, splashing in the waves, laughing and smiling, and so filled with joy wash through my head, so vivid. So crystal clear. As if it were a real memory instead of a fantasy that can never come true.

But that doesn't mean Ivy and their daughter are alone.

Never alone.

"She is going to know how much her father loved her, Ivy, because you're going to tell her every day. So will her grandmother and everyone else who knew Drew. And she's going to grow up with the best mom in the world, who's going to love her fiercely and protect her and give her everything she needs to thrive. You're going to do it." I feather my lips across her temple, wanting so badly to do so much more for her than merely give her words that may mean nothing. "You're going to be okay. I promise you that."

She shakes her head almost frantically, her hair brushing my face. "You don't know that."

I nod, pressing my lips to the top of her head again. "I do. Because you deserve it, Ivy. After everything you've suffered because of me, you deserve the world, and I wish I could give it to you. I wish I could give him back." That vise that wrapped around my chest the moment Drew died and has slowly tightened with each emotional blow somehow finds room to constrict even more, trying to steal my breath and words. But I need to say them. I *have* to get them out. "Every minute of every day, I think about it, Ivy. I think about that night and how differently I could have done things, how things should have gone. And how every single decision I made after that night was the wrong one. Not only for me, but for you, and for Drew. For this baby. For all of us. For the world. And now, I'm not the one *really* suffering the repercussions of it. You are, and I'm so fucking sorry for that."

It feels more like a goodbye than an apology.

Probably because it is.

This won't happen again.

She won't allow me to see her this vulnerable. She won't let me see her this weak. She will return to being the strong, stubborn Ivy who snatched that bottle from my hand and ensured I didn't flush all my hard work down the fucking toilet in a moment of desperation.

So, I bury my face in her hair again and just hold her, letting her cry as my own tears soak into her thick, dark strands. She tightens her grip on my hand, her fingers entwined with mine over her stomach, and we lie like that for what feels like an eternity.

In the dark, neither of us say anything to break the silence, and when her sobbing finally stops, her body finally still, I press a kiss to the top of her head again and start to slip away, but she tightens her hold on my hand.

"Please stay..."

Her request seems loud even though it's barely a whisper.

"You don't want that, Ivy."

She can't want that.

But she nods without looking at me. "I do. At least, right now."

She'll hate me again come morning.

And that's okay.

Right now, I have to give her what she needs, even if it kills me.

"I'd do anything for you, Ivy, give you anything you need. Anytime. Anywhere. Forever. All you have to do is ask."

"I'm asking you to stay..."

14

IVY

My eyelids flutter open to a dark, cold room.

He's gone.

I know it before I even fully wake from the best sleep I've had since I last slept in his arms. Back before I knew the truth...

Before I knew that he was responsible for Drew's death and all my anguish.

His leather and citrus scent lingers, but the warmth of his hard body at my back and his strong arm wrapped around me has been replaced by the chill of an empty bed.

The bed he said he would *never* get in before he ravished me in the kitchen like he was starving for something only I could give him.

My body instantly heats with the memory, but the baby kicks, quickly returning me to reality.

So much has changed since then...

I thought my world had ended when Drew died, but it turns out, things could still get worse. Every minute I spent with Cam slowly brought me back to life, reminded me that there were ways to find joy even in the torment.

And then it was snatched away from me...

All that *hope* that things would get better, that I might be able to find some sort of life without Drew that could offer me even a fraction of the love and contentment I had with him was crushed like the box the G.I. Joe doll arrived in.

That agony lives with me now, a constant reminder that things will never be okay again...despite what Cam tried to convince me of.

I'd rather go back to feeling numb like I did before Cam showed up than feel *this*. At least when I was floating in the nothingness, staring at the white wall of the bedroom, I could pretend everything wasn't so damn fucked up.

I could feel our daughter kick and imagine Drew coming home to me and doing the same, grinning and kissing my belly as he talked to her and experienced all that joy I know he would have at finally becoming a father.

It might not have been real, but that fantasy kept me from breaking.

It kept me from succumbing to the crushing weight of despair that sent me running from work early so I didn't crumble in front of Marlo and Trina—again.

But any chance of finding that magical, mythical place where things are *right* is as gone as Cam.

I force myself to roll to the side of the bed and climb out of it.

My gaze immediately sweeps to where he lay beside me, to a Post-it that now sits on the pillow.

I brought you dinner...
And something that belongs here.

Something that belongs here?

My stomach churns, reminding me I didn't eat dinner before Cam arrived, and I clench the note tightly in my fist, putting one foot in front of the other, slowly wandering down the hallway toward whatever waits from him.

As soon as my eyes land on the end table and what now rests beside the photo of Drew and me on the beach, any hope of holding back tears vanishes.

Gladys...

She stands in the new pot I moved her to that day Cam showed up, so many months ago, to apologize for how he barreled so unexpectedly into my life.

Looking strong and proud.

Healthy.

I managed to save her that day, to prevent her from withering away to the nothing it feels like I've become, yet I haven't been able to bring her home.

This space used to be filled with fresh flowers and plants, their vibrant colors and exquisite scents mirroring how blissful life seemed leading up to the wedding. But something about having such beautiful life in this house after Drew's death felt *wrong*.

Nothing should be that bright and happy when my world was as gray as Drew's ashes.

So, this place became a lifeless tomb even after I released what was left of him to the ocean. No plants. No flowers. No light. Just my hopelessness and pain. But as I absently rub my hand over my growing belly and move toward Mom's plant and my favorite photo of Drew and me together, the overwhelming grief I thought would hit me doesn't come.

It just looks *right*.

Like it always belonged in exactly this spot.

And Cam knew.

Even though we haven't spoken in months—save for the few strained words shared at the doctor's office and exchanged at the shore—he *knew* it was time to bring Gladys home and inject life back into the house before *this* little life comes kicking and screaming into it.

A single tear trickles down my cheek, and I wipe it away as I move to the kitchen and tug open the fridge to see what else he brought.

The plastic bag sits on the shelf, and I pull it out and set it on the counter with far too much trepidation.

Cam always seems to know what I need.

And he gives it to me even when I don't or can't ask for it.

And when I open it with shaking hands, I find another note on top.

I didn't know which one you might be craving.

I don't even have to open what's inside the cylindrical items wrapped in paper under the Post-it. Because I know what's inside—cheesesteaks from Max's and Dalessandro's.

15

CAM

*F*inally.

I don't know why it took me so long to get here. Nor can I understand why I struggled to figure out how to say what I've been trying to voice for so many fucking months.

It shouldn't have taken waking up in Drew's bed, with my arms wrapped around his fiancée, his baby kicking against my hand, to finally make me realize why everything I've painted has felt so fucking *wrong*.

But it did.

The moment I felt that tiny little foot press into my palm, I knew what I needed to do. I knew what I needed to *say*. And it needed to happen right away.

I move like a man possessed because that's what I am.

Only instead of being caught in an endless loop of sadness, that soul-crushing, monstrous force that seemed to churn and churn, spit me out, then suck me back into it again, I've finally gotten my head above water.

I'm consumed by the overwhelming need to get this *out* now that I understand.

All I've thought about is the *death* of everything I loved so much—Drew, my relationship with Mom, and this obsession with Ivy that only brought so much pain.

But that kick felt like *life.*

Because that's what it is.

That little girl *is* Drew.

And Drew *loved* life and all the things in it.

He fought day in and day out for other people's lives. To *save* them. To ensure their families never suffered the way we all are now. He loved even the simplest things— one in particular that we always shared.

The reason every time I picked up a brush and put paint on canvas has been so frustrating, so *infuriating,* was that I've been trying to tell the wrong story.

I've been *seeing* the wrong thing.

First, it was only Ivy...

Then Drew...

But it was the *wrong* Drew.

And now that it's so clear, I can't stop.

I couldn't even if I wanted to.

The image flows out of me so fast, so freely, that I don't even have to think about it. Because I've *lived* it. *We* lived it.

Black and white spreads across the pale bricks of the side of the building with focused, broad strokes and a steady hand...

It blends together into varying shades of gray, creating dimension that captures the memory so vividly that it could have happened yesterday instead of over twenty years ago.

The car headlights illuminate my progress in the otherwise darkened lot. Cold wind blows across my exposed skin, sending my hair flying wildly around my face, but I can't even feel the chill. The sounds of North Philly after midnight fill my ears—occasional cars on the street, laughter, yelling, the bark of a dog.

So many things that could be distracting...

Yet I block it all out easily.

One hundred percent of my focus falls on this wall.

This memory.

This *hope* I somehow feel the more the mural comes to life.

Because that's what I should have been doing this whole time since I lost Drew—focusing on his *life*. All those moments we shared that will remain embedded so deeply in my soul. Not his death and what it did to all of us.

And doing that meant going back to the beginning.

Coming here.

Doing this.

Because *this* was *us*.

16

IVY

The pounding on the front door draws me from bed far too early considering the mostly sleepless night I had after Cam left, and I groggily stumble to it, rubbing my eyes and yawning.

"Ivy!"

Marlo's muffled voice reaches me as I struggle to throw the lock with my brain still not quite completely awake.

"Hold on!" I finally manage to throw the deadbolt in the right direction and tug open the door to find her practically bouncing on the porch with the sun barely risen. "What are you doing here?"

And why the hell are you so damn perky this early?

She pushes past me, tugging her phone out of her pocket as she does. "Did you see the news this morning?"

"What?" I rub my eyes again, nudging the door closed with my hip. "No, you just woke me up—"

"Look!"

Blinking rapidly to clear my vision of those last remnants of sleep, I scan the headline of an article pulled up on her phone screen.

Cush Returns In Philly

My breath catches as I snatch it from her hand, quickly scrolling down to the image below the words. "Oh, my God..."

Marlo nods vigorously. "Right? That's them, isn't it?"

Them...

Tears blur my vision, and I have to swipe them away with my free hand to see the mural painted on pale brick. "Yeah, that's them..."

Right there in black and white.

So vivid and lifelike, it feels like I could reach out and touch the five-year-old versions of the two men who have altered my life in such immeasurable ways.

Drew and Cam...

Sitting on a curb...

In their matching outfits and shoes...

Sharing a cheesesteak...

My throat tightens, and I struggle to swallow through the clog that has lodged squarely in it as I stare at the painting of exactly what Cam described to me while we sat in that booth at Max's.

God, was that really only a few months ago?

It seems impossible to believe when so much has happened since then, when so many things that are so huge have changed in such a short period of time.

The baby kicks, almost as if she's sensing my heightened emotions and is responding in kind.

I rub gently at the spot and glance up at Marlo. "Where is this?"

She snags the phone from my hand and scrolls down through the written article to another photo of the mural taken from farther back. "On a building behind Max's parking lot. It appeared overnight." Her wide eyes scan over the screen, her lips parted in awe. "I mean, he must have been up all night painting that—"

"No." I shake my head, my body trembling as everything that happened last night replays through my mind. "It wasn't all night."

Because I woke up to him gone well before midnight.

The bed was already cold.

Which means he must have left here to go do *this*.

Hot tears trail down my cheeks, and Marlo grabs my wrist, dragging my attention back to her rather than what any of this means.

Her brow furrows. "What do you mean?"

Pulling free from her hold, I stumble to the couch and drop down onto it, afraid my legs won't continue to hold me up. "He was here..."

Marlo looks from me to Gladys sitting on the end table. "I figured he was at some point. He stopped by with dinner and was worried when I told you you had already left." She trails her fingers around the edge of the pot. "And he saw Gladys and wanted to bring her to you."

A smile tugs at my lips. "Yeah, he...uh...stayed for a while."

Her eyes widen. "What's *a while*?"

Shit.

I bury my face in my hands, embarrassment heating my cheeks. "I'm not totally sure. I fell asleep, but I woke up hungry around maybe eleven, and he was gone..."

She drops onto the couch beside me, narrowing her assessing gaze and likely seeing far too much. "What's wrong?"

So many things.

All those reasons I was lying in that bed alone, staring at the wall, trying to escape into a fantasy because reality was crippling yesterday still exist.

That agony that made me break down in front of Cam when I promised myself I would never give him a reason to worry because I *needed* him out of my life still lives in my chest.

Drew is still gone, and *we're* still here, facing a future without him.

But as I rest my hand over my stomach and rub at the spot where the baby likes to press her foot, the emptiness I felt when I woke to Cam gone doesn't seem so... fathomless.

And I don't know what to do with that.

Just like I've never known what to do with this hurricane of conflicting emotions Camden Usher created when he stormed into my life unexpectedly.

The raging pregnancy hormones don't help anything.

It seems like anything and everything can set off a downward spiral that I'm not capable of pulling myself out of alone. I probably wouldn't have been able to if Cam hadn't shown up last night, if he hadn't said those words and made those promises I want so badly to believe.

I shake my head to try to clear away those thoughts that will pull me down the dark path I somehow escaped. "Nothing is wrong. This is..." My gaze travels to her phone still clutched in her hand, the mural still up on the screen. A long breath rushes from my lungs. "This is a good thing. And I want to see it."

Marlo nods, pushing to her feet and sliding her phone into her pocket. "Let's go."

"Now?"

She sighs and holds out a hand to me. "Yes, now. Trina can open alone today." A grin pulls at her lips. "We need to see this in person."

It's even more stunning up close.

From here, I can see every minute detail Cam included in the image. So perfect that it's like a snapshot in time. Yet he somehow did it with only black and white.

The way one brother closes his eyes as he takes a bite, as if he can't wait to savor it, while the other grips the sandwich with both hands, ready to devour it, makes it so easy to tell which one is Drew.

He savored life.

Never took it for granted.

Lived each moment with the kind of intense love of it that mirrored the way he loved me.

But Cam...

He *devours*.

Anything and anyone in his path.

He sees something he wants, and he consumes.

That's precisely what he did with me, and staring at this image now, surrounded by dozens of strangers who came to see it, too, I somehow *know* this was meant for me as much as it was for him.

This mural is a love letter to his brother and an apology for everything that went wrong between them.

It was the only way he could say it.

Tears spill down my cheeks, and Marlo wraps her arm around me and squeezes.

"You good?"

I shake my head. "Not really."

My hands move down to rub at my stomach, where the baby's movements seem to have only increased since we arrived, almost as if she's as excited as I was to see this.

That's your daddy...

And your uncle...

The memory of his large, warm hand pressed against the same spot mine now rests, and the way he held me so tightly through my complete breakdown, threatens to buckle my knees.

But Marlo's hold on me keeps me steady.

"What do I do?"

I glance over at her, and she offers me a sympathetic half-smile.

"I've never known you not to do the right thing, Ivy."

A little half-laugh, half-sob slips from my lips. "But what if I don't know what the right thing is?" I shake my head. "I can't...I can't stop *hating* him and being so fucking *angry* about what he's caused. How am I supposed to forgive that?"

Marlo's gaze cuts to the mural, and she stares at it for a

long time before she finally returns her focus to me. "I don't know. Maybe you don't?"

"And keep him from his niece's life?"

From mine?

It's the last thing I should want after everything that's happened, but I can't deny that last night, the thought that he might not stay, that he might turn and walk away instead, had filled me with so much fear that it physically hurt.

Or that waking up and finding him gone felt like losing something important all over again.

But I also can't deny this bone-deep anger I continue to carry with me every day at how things have turned out.

This baby will never know the man on this wall. She won't know his laughter, or his gentle touch, or feel how much he loves her the way I always did.

And there's only *one* reason for that.

One person to blame.

The identical little boy sitting next to him, who somehow always manages to break through the walls I build around myself and make me question everything.

Just like he is doing right now.

17

CAM

I shouldn't be here.

I shouldn't be intruding.

I shouldn't be letting myself in—uninvited—yet again.

I shouldn't keep inserting myself into her life.

Especially after what happened last night...

But that's exactly why I'm here again.

Because seeing her that way, knowing how much she must have been suffering to want me to stay so badly, to *need* that so much from *me*, of all people, means I haven't been able to stop worrying about her all day.

This boulder of dread has sat in my stomach since I got home from painting the mural just before dawn broke, and nothing I did has been able to shake it.

Not a long, hot shower to attempt to wash away her scent while I scrubbed the paint from my skin.

Not smoking half a fucking pack of cigarettes.

Not pacing the studio until my bare feet ached.

It wasn't until I turned onto her street that the unease finally started to ebb, that it finally felt like I could breathe again because I knew I would see her soon—even if that isn't what she wants.

I push open the front door, bag with her dinner in hand, and pause, tilting my head and listening for her.

She's usually home by now...

And I was half-expecting her to be sitting on the couch, waiting for me.

To tell me what a mistake last night was.

To remind me how much she hates me.

But there isn't any sign of her, save for her purse sitting on the counter just inside the door that leads to the garage and her shoes on the floor near it, like she came in and kicked them off haphazardly.

The way I found her last night flashes through my head, and my gut tightens as hard as my hand does around the bag.

Is she in bed again, practically catatonic?

Leaving her was one of the hardest things I ever had to do, but if she had woken and I was still in her bed—in *their* bed—wrapped around her, it would have only complicated things even more for both of us.

And I had to paint.

I *had* to get that *out* after all this time, or I would have imploded.

Still, the guilt remains.

At walking away when she still needed me...

She may need you tonight.

That little voice whispers as I set the bag on the counter and proceed down the hall toward the bedroom.

Each step that draws me closer to the open door only amps up the apprehension over what I might find.

If she's like that again...

But the rumpled bed is empty.

Her scent permeates the room, though—that sweet, floral smell that can act like a soothing balm for my soul or attack it violently depending on the mental state I find myself in when it hits me.

Tonight, it brings tears to my eyes that mirror those we both shed last night, and when an all too familiar sound draws my attention across the room to the closed bathroom door, they finally fall.

A sob.

Filled with anger, frustration, and anguish.

One I recognize all too well.

Ivy has cried enough tears to fill the world's oceans a hundred times over, and no matter how much I want it, how many times I pray to God for it, they aren't going to stop.

And I'm the reason her world has fallen apart.

I'm the reason she's here, alone and pregnant, when Drew should be at her side through what should be the most joyful time of their lives.

Which is why I should turn around and leave.

I know deep down that it's the right thing to do, yet I rub at the sharp ache in my chest and slowly move toward the closed bathroom door. Now that I'm closer, I can hear the water running in the shower, mixing with the sounds of her distress.

Just like it always seems to where Ivy is concerned, memories overwhelm me. Her pain last night, mixing and twisting together with the feel of holding her in *my* shower, of washing her smooth skin clean after I fucked her on the canvas.

My ribcage tightens until I can barely draw in a breath.

Fuck...

I press my hands flat against the wooden panel and lower my forehead to it, listening to the sound of the rushing water and Ivy's sobs.

Tears trail down my cheeks.

My stomach turns.

I want to go to her.

I want to make sure she's all right.

I want to take her into my arms the way I did last night and offer her *whatever* it is she needs to make it through the night.

But I can't.

Her sobs only increase the longer I stand frozen by regret and indecision. Each tortured sound that floats through the door hurts more and more until I'm trembling violently to hold myself back from running to her.

Something clatters hard against the tiles, and I jerk my head from the door, my heart racing as worry twists around my spine and forces my hand.

I turn the handle and push it in without considering what I'm doing. If she's pissed at me for being here, I'll take anything she throws at me. Because anger is better than her agony.

"Ivy? Are you all right?"

A wall of steam hits me immediately, but as I step in

through it, the vision beyond the glass separating us robs me of the ability to see anything but *her.*

Standing in the shower, water cascading over her smooth skin, face buried in her hands, as sobs continue to wrack her body. "Ivy?"

She doesn't react.

Doesn't respond to my abrupt intrusion or questions.

Oh, God...

Acid climbs up my throat.

What if it's the baby?

I rush forward and slide open the glass door, frantically scanning for any evidence of blood or anything that might tell me what's happening since Ivy seems incapable.

A razor and bottle of shaving cream lie on the tile at her feet, but as I scan up her legs and over her naked body, the only thing that appears to be wrong is the way mine reacts to her.

"Ivy..." My voice wavers, all the anxious energy I'm incapable of containing leeching out in my words. "You need to tell me you're okay."

The water continues to fall over her, running in rivulets down her naked body, across her full breasts and protruding belly, between her legs...the sound of it hitting the tile the only thing that breaks the silence.

Slowly, she lifts her face out of her hands, her eyes swollen, her lips trembling, her thick, dark hair plastered down her back and her shoulders. "I can't do it..."

"What?"

She could be referencing a thousand different things: going on without Drew, having this baby without him...

but another sob slips from her lips instead of an answer, and she squeezes her eyes closed, shaking her head. "I tried, and I just *can't.*"

One of her hands slides to her distended belly, and I follow the movement, remembering what it felt like to have my palm pressed there last night, to feel that tiny, fluttering kick, to know the life growing inside her is the miracle she and Drew always hoped for.

"Is the baby okay?"

I hold my breath waiting for the answer, a silent prayer held in my heart.

Please, God, let her be okay...

Ivy nods, trying to control her breathing through her sobs, but they only seem to get worse. Gasping, short pants and a heaving chest that terrifies me for more than one reason. Whatever she's so upset about, if she doesn't get herself under control, she's going to hyper-ventilate.

Shit.

I toe off my shoes, tug off my socks, and step into the shower before I can question the sanity of the action. The flow from the showerhead soaks me instantly, but it wouldn't matter if it were fucking acid—nothing is going to stop me from getting to her.

But I won't risk doing anything that might upset her further by touching her when she's like this, so close to tipping over the edge of something so dangerous. Something I recognize all too well.

"Ivy..." Only a few inches from her now, the scent of her shampoo and soap fills my lungs along with that floral smell that always clings to her. "Look at me."

It takes a few seconds before she lifts her eyes and does it.

"Tell me what's wrong." I try to keep my voice level, but my desperation slips out. *"Please."*

Because the longer she takes to answer, to explain what the hell is happening, the harder it's becoming to remain calm, like she needs me to be.

Water beats down on us, steam rising to fill the thick air heavy with unspoken words and a swirling storm of emotions that always seems to exist when we're in each other's orbit.

She sniffles, inhaling a few sharp breaths, and her hand motions down absently. "I haven't shaved in weeks." Her lips tremble, like she's struggling to keep herself together enough to speak. "I feel like a goddamn sasquatch. And I just wanted to do it, but"—she sobs again, clenching her eyes closed—"I can't reach right and then I dropped everything, and the thought of bending down to pick it up just—"

Another anguished sound echoes around us, cutting off her explanation.

Shit...

I release a relieved rush of air from my lungs that's also filled with guilt at feeling that way. But the current situation is far more manageable than the thousand other worst-case scenarios I had worked up in my head.

She's overwhelmed. Clearly upset and at her breaking point. But she's *fine.*

Physically, she's *okay.*

And so is the baby.

But her tears continue as do her heaving breaths, as if

not being able to shave her legs is the worst she's been through in the last several months, instead of all the horrific things she's experienced, and my heart shatters for her for the millionth time.

"Ivy? You're okay."

She shakes her head. "I'm not."

But you can make it okay for her...

There are so many things I can't fix, so many things that can't be undone, but *this* I can do.

Or at least, I can *try*.

I sink to my knees in front of her, reaching for the shaving cream, her swollen belly mere inches from my face.

"Cam"—her unsteady voice floats to me over the rushing water—"what are you doing?"

Something I probably shouldn't.

I glance up at her as I pull the top off the shaving cream and spread some on my hand. "What does it look like I'm doing?"

Her eyes widen, her soft lips parting. "You...you can't."

Shouldn't.

Not can't.

I hold her gaze even if it means she can see how strongly being this close to her is affecting me. Because it most definitely is. It would be impossible to be near this woman naked, wet, and so fucking beautiful like this with her stomach full with new life. "Let me help you, Ivy. You can hate me all you want after, I promise."

She sucks in another sharp breath, watching as I gently run my hands up and down her legs, coating them in the shaving cream and desperately trying not to notice how she reacts to my touch.

Her body tenses, then starts trembling so hard I have to grip her thigh to keep it steady.

Our gazes stay locked for a moment, until I'm forced to look away to break the intensity of it that might make me say or do something foolish.

I pull my hands from her skin and rinse them before grabbing the razor and glancing back up at her. "Don't move."

Because I don't have a fucking clue what I'm doing.

I've never shaved a woman before, and the way my hands are shaking, I probably shouldn't even be attempting it right now. Because if I hurt her more than I already have, I don't think I could survive it.

She bites her bottom lip as she watches me, and I press the razor against her right ankle and slowly glide it up, holding my breath the entire time.

Somehow, I manage to make it up the smooth expanse of her thigh without breaking skin, and I release a relieved breath as I finally pull it away to rinse it under the water pounding against my back.

I rinse off the razor and shave another strip.

And another.

Another.

With each one, I grow a little less worried that I'm going to maim her, and I cautiously make my way around one leg, then the other. Trying to concentrate on keeping my strokes long and slow rather than the aggressive, determined ones I use when painting—or fucking.

Ivy trembles, her muscles tensing and quivering

directly in front of my face in a way that ignites heat in very inappropriate places.

She's very wet.

And very naked.

And *incredibly* fucking beautiful.

And right in front of me.

So fucking close I could lean an inch and have my face buried in her sweet cunt.

But that isn't what this is about.

It's about ending her distress, offering her what I can, even when it's woefully inadequate.

Another apology in the only way I know how to offer it...

When I'm finally done and have washed the remnants of the shaving cream off her smooth skin, I look up at her and offer the tiniest smile.

She lets her lip fall from between her teeth and glances down, but I know she can't see much of anything because of her growing stomach. Her hand drifts to the dark thatch of hair at the apex of her legs, and air catches in my throat on a strangled groan.

Fuck...

I swallow thickly and stare up at her. Water clings to her thick, dark lashes, but I can't tell whether it's from the shower or her tears.

Likely a combination of both.

But—at least for the moment—her tears have stopped.

Only what's replaced them is even more dangerous.

Another distressing need swims in her heated gaze.

I rest my hand over hers, skimming my thumb

through the hair covering her pussy. "Do you want me to shave you here, too?"

The tiniest whimper slips from her lips, and she nods.

Sweet. Fuck.

Ivy knows what she's asking, yet she's asking it anyway.

I let out a long breath, trying to stop my heart from pounding and my hands from trembling before I take on this monumentally stupid task.

Of all the dumb things I've done in my life, this has to be right near the top of the list.

Because touching her like this will completely undo me.

I'm barely hanging on by a thread as it is, and after last night, my body craves this woman more than I ever thought possible.

But I somehow manage to rein myself in enough to tap the top of the bench to my right. "Put your leg up here."

She nods and lifts her foot there, spreading herself open and fully exposing her cunt to me.

My hard cock twitches in the confines of my jeans, now *far* too tight.

Fucking. Hell.

Even like this, near the verge of emotional breakdown, she's still beautiful.

The scent of her arousal mingles with that of the shaving cream as I lean in and spread it across that most sacred place. My fingers brush over her mound, the crease between her pelvis and thighs, and down across her pussy lips, making her twitch in my hold.

I still my hand and glance up at her, but her eyes are closed, head tipped back against the tile wall.

And I know that look.

It's the same one I saw before I railed her on the canvas.

When I pulled her leg over my shoulder and tasted her...

Fuck.

Fuck.

Fuck.

The emotions warring inside me fight for supremacy —the part of me that has always been so fucking addicted to this woman begging for me to *take* while my head keeps telling me to give her what she needs.

But neither of those things can happen.

Not now.

Not ever again.

I grab the razor and get to work, worried about what my hands might do if I don't have something in them. Slowly and methodically, I shave every inch of her skin until she's completely smooth and my cock leaks.

Her legs tremble, her hands pressed flat to the tile as if she's struggling to keep herself up, and when I finally pull back, she opens her eyes and looks down at me with absolute heat burning in them that has nothing to do with the temperature of the water or the steam filling the air.

She needs something more than help with *this.*

She needs something she's afraid to ask for because we both know it's a terrible idea to cross that line again.

I set down the razor, rinsing my hands but never taking my eyes off her. "I told you I'd do anything for you,

Ivy. Give you anything you need. Anytime. Anywhere. Forever. That all you had to do was ask..."

She shifts restlessly but keeps her leg up on the bench, spread open directly in front of my face like a goddamn gift from a god who wants to torture me in the worst way possible—with the *one* thing I should never touch again. "Please, Cam."

The waver in her voice makes mine come out harsher, filled with all the reservations keeping me frozen in place. "Please what?"

Her gaze stays locked on mine, her determination darkening it as her hips roll forward in offering. "Make me come. Make me forget. Make me..." A droplet of water slides down her cheek, and this time, I'm confident it's a tear because her voice cracks with her plea. "Make it okay."

18

CAM

Nothing ever *could*, ever *will*, make *any* of this okay.

We both know that.

My lie to her, my betrayal of Drew, all of it lives in that realm of *this will never be okay...*

There aren't enough apologies or acts that could make up for it, but I meant what I said to her with every fiber of my being. I may have failed her at every opportunity to do the right thing in the past, but I will be here for her now. For the future. For whatever she needs. Any time, any place, any thing, for as long as she lets me. Even if she continues to hate me.

And I can do this for her now, give her what she needs, even if it destroys me in the process.

I stare up at her, the water sluicing over her swollen breasts and stomach, then sliding down her legs to the tiles where I still kneel—a man ready and willing to worship the only person who has ever truly deserved it.

Ivy's meltdown wasn't about shaving.

She's suffered so much over the last several months, and everything has compounded until she reached this breaking point. Last night was a step in this direction, and I somehow managed to hold her together long enough to get *here*.

But there isn't any way to roll it back and pretend none of it happened.

There isn't enough water to wash away the *look* she's giving me or to quench the thirst I have for her.

So, I will do what she wants, even if it's going to hurt me brutally in the end.

I slide my hands up the inside of her thighs slowly, giving her every chance to end this, to close herself off to me in every way, but instead of doing that, she trembles under my touch, goosebumps breaking out on her skin, despite the hot water and the steam in the air.

Her gaze stays locked with mine as I caress her flesh, relishing the way it moves under my touch, how responsive she is to every scrape of my callouses and sweep of my fingertips.

No matter how badly things have ended up between us, no matter how big the chasm that separates us and makes what I really want impossible, there's no denying an electric current still sparks between us. So real. So physical. So alive, despite every reason it should have died when she learned the truth.

It ripples through me now as I caress her skin, and Ivy pulls her bottom lip under her teeth, biting down as her hands splay against the tiles in anticipation.

And I can't make her wait any longer.

Wrapping my hands around her thighs to hold her steady, I dip my head and drag my tongue through her core.

Fuuuuuck.

She groans, her head dropping to the tile with a soft *thunk*. And I can't help the rumble of satisfaction that rattles through my chest at the taste of her arousal, at the taste of *her* coating my tongue and sliding down my throat.

I've missed it so fucking much.

I've dreamed about it and craved this so badly that it became abundantly clear that Ivy truly *is* a drug to me.

Since the moment I got my first taste of her that night in the garden, I was violently addicted.

Willing to do *anything* to get my next fix.

Unable to shake the driving need to taste color again and let it infect my world.

Kissing her lips tasted like *red*, and licking her cunt is like having the entire fucking rainbow flashing across my eyes for the first time since I was a child.

My achingly hard cock strains against my zipper, throbbing and pulsing because it would be impossible not to want to be inside her right now. With my face buried between her thighs and my tongue deep in her cunt, the memory of driving into her, of having her come apart around me, is almost too much to bear.

But I will never make this about me.

Never again.

It's about what Ivy needs.

Release.

From all those things that forced her into that bed last

night, that compelled her to seek my arms, that made her fall apart over a damn razor, that demanded she ask for *this*.

I glide my tongue up across her clit, making her jerk in my hold. My fingers dig into her fleshy thighs, and she slaps her left hand against the tile, her right burying in my hair.

She grips it tightly and holds me in place, grinding her hips to my face, seeking control over *something* when she lacks it in every other aspect of her life right now.

Releasing another groan of approval, I bury my tongue inside her as deeply as I can, needing to fill her, to complete her, to consume her.

Her strangled gasp makes my heart falter, and she tugs on my hair, trying to direct me, but she doesn't have to because I know what she wants.

I understand it.

She needs it quick and hard.

This isn't a game, like she accused me of playing that night she learned the truth and walked away.

This isn't about toying with her or taking my own pleasure from devouring her endlessly.

That would be something the old Camden would do.

The one who made too many mistakes to count because he was a self-centered asshole who only cared about one thing—getting what *he* wanted.

I made a promise to myself that day in the doctor's office that I would never make a selfish decision again, especially not when it comes to this woman or this baby.

I've already cost them too much.

Cost *everyone* too much.

And I'm done making them pay the price for my failures.

I'm done making her *wait*.

I glide my hand up her thigh and slip a finger inside her as my tongue flicks across her clit ruthlessly. She gasps, her pussy contracting around me, my cock aching in the same rhythm I pump up in her.

Her hips start moving against my face more frantically as I slide another finger into her, stretching her wider. A satisfied moan echoes off the tile, urging me onward, and I continue to attack that bundle of nerves at the apex of her thighs relentlessly as I thrust up into her, curling my fingertips into that soft spot, deep inside her that I know will send her chasing down her release.

Ivy tips her head back and to the side, partially allowing me to see her around her belly. With her lips slightly parted, short, breathless pants slipping from between them, she looks so fucking stunning that all I can see is how it would look on a canvas.

Frozen forever in time.

All I want to do is make her come and capture the moment in my head so I can paint it, so she can see how stunning she is, even in her despair, even when it feels like her world is falling apart.

Her grip on my hair tightens the harder I thrust my fingers into her and the faster my tongue moves across her engorged clit. The water beating down on us has nothing on the rush of arousal dripping from her cunt and into my greedy mouth. And I swallow it down. Savoring every drop. As desperate for it as she is for her release.

My free hand grips her hips as they buck and roll,

fucking my face so wildly that I can barely breathe, completely smothered by her desire. But this woman can use me any way she wants, for as long as she wants, even if it kills me.

I deserve everything coming my way, and the way she moves against me, grinding down almost violently on my mouth and tongue and fingers, it wouldn't surprise me if she has every intent to suffocate me with her cunt.

Her pussy clenches around my fingers, needy and seeking more, and I push a third one into her, spreading her even wider. A sharp gasp fills the shower, bouncing off the tile surrounding us, and the sound makes my hips jerk forward, the memory of her making it as I entered her enough to almost make me come on the spot.

I nip at her wet flesh and suck her clit between my lips in a pulsing rhythm that matches my thrusts into her, and she finally explodes.

The cry that rips from deep in her chest vibrates through me as her body jerks in my hold. Her hips roll, riding the wave of pleasure that courses through her. I wrap my arm around her waist, holding her steady through the ride, continuing to pump into her and drag the orgasm out as long as I can.

She seems to ride it forever.

Tears leak from my eyes as I watch her.

Because this will be the last time I ever get to see it.

Because she'll come to her senses.

Once this euphoria wears off, she'll realize what a mistake she made by allowing me to touch her like this.

She'll regret it, the same way she regrets every moment we ever spent together.

And when that happens, I'll be left with nothing more than these fleeting memories and moments of beauty to get me through the dark and lonely nights.

So, I'll relish every second of it, savor every drop that coats my tongue and throat, and take as much of her in as I can before she pushes me away.

Her grip on my hair finally loosens, and she sags into me, forcing me to pull my face back. But I am nowhere near done with her. I dip my head to lick off the arousal from her inner thighs, needing every drop of it, every last taste.

She sags, trembling violently with her leg still braced up on the bench, and I tighten my hold on her, keeping her upright as my tongue glides across her skin. Time ticks by slowly as I clean her thoroughly, but eventually, I have to pull my fingers from inside her.

Hooded, lust-hazed eyes follow as I lift them to my mouth and lick them, then ease her foot down to the tile. Her eyes slide closed, and Ivy wavers slightly, hand still buried in my hair, the other slapped against the wall like she needed that to ground her so she wouldn't fly away. Her chest heaves with each ragged breath, and the hot water beats down on my shoulders as I examine every inch of her.

All those changes the pregnancy has made to her body that have made her even more stunning.

I'd give anything to be able to witness the color of her skin, to watch the pinks and reds spread across it rather than merely being able to see the slight variations of gray.

I know it would be breathtaking.

Because everything about her is.

She finally lifts her head again, and her eyes flutter open to meet mine.

The stormy gaze isn't filled with the hate I expect to see, but now, I know it wasn't just water trailing down her cheeks, because tears shimmer and trickle from the corner of her eyes as she stares down at me.

I stay on my knees before her, the only place I belong, because this woman deserves to be worshipped.

She deserved Drew and everything he gave her.

What she doesn't deserve is a fuck-up like me, yet I can't seem to stay away.

And neither can she, even when she doesn't want it.

Finally, her grip on my hair releases, and she pulls her shaking hand back.

It continues to tremble as she presses it over her belly.

I hold her gaze, ensuring she's with me before I say what she needs to hear, what needs to be said—for both of us. "Keep hating me, Ivy. You need to. I know you do, and it's okay. But I'm going to make you that same promise again. Anything you want, anything you need, any time. I'll give it to you."

A sob rips from her throat, and I want to push to my feet and pull her into my arms, to absorb all her pain and carry that weight so she doesn't have to anymore.

But I know it isn't what she wants.

It isn't what she needs.

She needs to not see Drew's face and know that it's all my fault he's not here.

She needs to pretend I don't exist, even after what just happened between us.

I push to my feet, keeping my arm wrapped around

her since I'm not confident her unsteady legs will keep her upright. Her hand on her belly, now pinned against my soaked shirt, flexes, and I stare down at her, tilting her chin up to make sure she looks at me.

"*Anything*, Ivy. All you have to do is ask."

If what just happened doesn't prove to her that I mean my words, nothing will...

I step back, though it takes every ounce of self-control I possess to do it.

The last thing I want is to leave her like this—or leave her at *all*. Ever. For the rest of my fucking life, I would stay on my knees and beg for this woman's forgiveness.

But that isn't an option.

That isn't the reality.

I slide open the shower door and step out onto the mat, soaked to the bone, dripping wet, with my heart in my throat and my cock straining in my jeans.

She watches me as I snag a towel from the rack and run it over my hair and face, then unbutton my shirt and tug it off. I wipe down my chest, then wrap the soaked clothes in the towel.

But I don't dare touch the waistband of my jeans or the zipper, because if I do, I might be tempted to do something with my hard, aching cock, like take it in my hand as I have so many fucking times over the years thinking about this woman.

She needs me to go.

And I need to leave.

It takes every ounce of willpower I possess to turn away from her, bend down, grab my socks and shoes, and stalk toward the door in my soaked jeans with my cock begging me to go back.

I pause just outside the bathroom door and glance at her—looking seriously well-pleasured and yet somehow distraught, standing in the exact same spot I left her. "Sorry about the water on your floor."

And so many other things.

19

IVY

Hours have passed since Cam disappeared out the bathroom door.

His wet footprints dried from the floor before I even managed to pull myself off the bench in the shower, where I collapsed and sat for God only knows how long after he left.

The only evidence he was here is the way my legs still tremble, the food in the fridge, and the bag of bright red fruit sitting on the counter.

The baby is as big as a pomegranate at 21 weeks. They're one of my favorite fruits. Try them with the vanilla Greek yogurt.

Dammit...

Tears blur his words, making them impossible to read

anymore, but nothing can wash away this feeling that settles squarely in my chest each week when I find his notes.

Because it's precisely the type of thing Drew would be doing if he were here...

Tracking the weeks and the size of the baby.

Ensuring I'm eating even when I don't feel well.

Taking care of me the way he did in the shower...

And I'm lying to myself when I say he didn't leave something else when he walked out—a reopened gaping wound in my chest.

It was created when Drew died.

When the love of my life was ripped away from me without warning and with no explanation.

It almost killed me.

Every second, every minute, every hour felt like I was bleeding out without Drew.

But then I opened that door to the storm churning outside, and I saw *him*.

The man who shared his face but has proven to be so different in so many ways.

Cam somehow helped hold those shredded pieces of my heart together.

His constant strength and unyielding presence gave me what I didn't even know I needed in those moments—someone to share my grief with and who understood what I was suffering.

He gave me something to cling to when I felt like I couldn't keep going.

But after everything that's happened, that wound he helped heal has reopened.

It festers inside me the same way my grief and anger do.

And what just happened in that shower, what I'm staring at through my tears on this counter, only make the pain worse.

20

CAM
TWO DAYS LATER

Dale drums his fingers on the side of his coffee mug, his dark eyes locked on me where I sit across from him in the booth at the diner near my studio. The same place Ivy came after we spent our first night together—which seems fitting for why we're meeting this morning.

And I know that look.

He's given it to me before, times he thought I was making bad decisions that might lead me to pick up again.

But this time, it's even more intense.

I should have expected it after the confession I just made.

Telling him what happened the other night with Ivy and explaining to him how badly it left me rattled after I walked away from her, soaking wet and confused as fuck, exposed something he's been saying all along—*she* is my biggest trigger.

My sweetest obsession and what could be my biggest downfall.

I run my hand through my hair and release a long sigh to break the tension permeating the air. "Just say it."

The corners of his lips twitch. "You already know what I'm going to say."

"It doesn't mean you don't want to say it yourself, Dale."

He smirks, relaxing back into the booth and sliding his arm across the red pleather. "I've been around the block more times than I can count, kid, and I'm going to tell you, whether you want to hear it or not, that what you are doing is incredibly dangerous to your recovery."

I snort. "You think I don't know that?"

A dark brow raises at me. "Then why are you still doing it?"

Fuck.

Because I'm a masochist.

Because I can't imagine turning my back and walking away *for good* from the woman I love, who is going to give birth to my niece soon.

Because maybe I am still that selfish person I've been trying so hard *not* to be.

I bury my face in my hands and release a long, frustrated groan that I feel in every cell of my body. When I lift my head again, he's still watching me, waiting for an answer. "Because what else am I supposed to do, Dale? Just walk away from her?"

His brow rises again, and he nods. "Yes."

I throw up my hands. "I can't fucking do that, Dale. She's pregnant with my niece. My mom and I are the only people she has left to help her through this pregnancy and everything that comes after it."

"What about her friends?" He waves a hand. "Uhhh... Marlo and somebody. Trina?"

"She was her mom's best friend."

He raises his palms. "There you go! She has people. People who love her, people who are going to support her and take care of her, people who aren't fucking *triggered* by her."

I glower at him.

"What? You know as well as I do that that woman is your trigger. Not *one* of them; she's *it*. Period. End of story. All the guilt and pain you feel that makes you want to pick up again stems from what started with *her* the night you first met. All the actions you took after that were tied to *her*. You look back and don't even recognize that person who did those things because you were in the throes of addiction. Both to drugs and whatever dopamine your system was creating where Ivy was concerned. Then, the guilt over your actions sent you spiraling again. But in the end, it's always been about her, hasn't it?"

It has.

But it doesn't mean I want to hear that the only way to keep myself level is to leave her when she's in such a vulnerable state.

My hand shakes on top of the table, my knee bouncing wildly under it.

I need a fucking cigarette...

"Don't look at me like that, Cam. You asked me to be your sponsor because, and I quote, I 'always give it to you straight.'" He leans forward slightly, gripping his mug.

"Even when you don't want to hear it. And right now, what you need to hear is that you need to walk away from her. Let your mom play grandmother and step into that role and do what needs to be done. Let her friends support her. What you don't need to be doing is going over there and going down on that woman."

"Jesus, Dale..."

I glance around the diner to ensure nobody heard him, and the waitress approaches with our meals in time to force me to hold back what I was about to say to him.

"Here you go." She sets my breakfast in front of me, but the plate full of eggs, bacon, toast, and potatoes suddenly doesn't look as appetizing as it sounded when I ordered it.

Dale, however, grabs his silverware and dives right into his steak and eggs, slicing them up as soon as she walks away while he glances at me. He pauses with his knife mid-air. "What? Are we pretending that isn't what happened?"

I run my hand through my hair again and shake my head. "No, that's exactly what happened, but you don't have to sound so...judgmental about it. You should have seen her, Dale..." My chest tightens picturing how distraught she was. The pain and frustration in her eyes when I opened that shower still haunt me. "She was hysterical. A complete mess. She was breaking, and I couldn't just stand there and watch that happen to her."

His brow furrows, the lines there deepening. "Why not? Why do you always have to be the one who comes to her rescue? Why couldn't you have called Marlo, or Trina, or even your mother to come over?"

Fuck.

He isn't wrong about that.

Any of them would have been at the house in twenty minutes if I had called, and they would have figured out a way to calm her and get her through the breakdown moment.

But that would have been twenty minutes too long.

"You know why."

He finishes chewing the food in his mouth and swallows. "Because you love her?"

I give him a sharp nod.

How could I stand there, watching the woman I love suffer so much and not do something *to help? How could I leave, knowing she would have to wait twenty more minutes like that to have someone hold her and comfort her?*

"Do you, though?"

His question stiffens my spine, my blood running icy cold. "What the fuck kind of a question is that?"

He points his fork at me. "The kind you should actually be asking yourself if you haven't already, and I don't think you have. You've been obsessed with this woman for over four years, Cam. And *obsessed* is the right word. You let her take control of everything about your life; you let your feelings for her destroy your relationship with your brother, who was your best friend and the closest person to you. You let it destroy your relationship with your mother because you couldn't come clean about why you and Drew were fighting. When you couldn't have her, you turned to alcohol and drugs to try to deaden the pain and guilt over what you had done. And it was all based on a lie you told her that night by pretending to be your brother.

Is that any way to start any sort of relationship? Does that sound healthy to you?"

"Fuck you, Dale."

He holds up his hands, still clutching his silverware between his fingers. "I'm playing devil's advocate here. Literally my job. This woman triggers you in every way possible, and if you continue to stay in her life, you're going to continue to get dragged into these highly emotional situations that are very likely to push you toward picking up."

Dale shoves another bite into his mouth and chews, giving me a moment to think about his warning.

I cringe as the memory of holding the heroin in my hand and twisting the cap off that bottle of whiskey flickers through my head.

It's the last thing I want to do, the last place I ever want to find myself again.

He swallows and takes a sip of his coffee. "You also know that it isn't just *bad* emotions that can trigger a relapse, Cam. You could finally be *happy* because you got what you always wanted, but *that* could be just as dangerous as all those other emotions."

Dale is right.

He usually is.

That's why I wanted him as my sponsor—because he has been clean for almost three decades but relapsed several times before getting to that point. He's been through it all and understands triggers better than anyone.

Except this isn't just a trigger.

This is a *person.*

This is someone who is family forever now because of the baby growing inside of her.

"You're asking me to walk away from my family."

He pauses with a bite of steak halfway up to his mouth. "Are they your family, or are they Drew's?"

I cringe, squeezing my eyes closed at the pain that lashes through my chest. "They're Drew's."

The words hurt to say even more than they do to hear.

"And is it your responsibility to pick up the pieces? Or should Ivy be able to find a life without you and the memories of everything that happened constantly surrounding her?"

I want to tell him that isn't fair, but he's right.

As much as she might be a trigger for me, I am for her, too.

Every time she sees me, every time we talk, when I touch her the way I did two nights ago, it all brings this rush of conflicting emotions barreling back like a tidal wave that threatens to pull me under the dark water.

"So...you're saying I should walk away."

He shoves the steak into his mouth. "That's exactly what I'm saying. It's my job to help you through your recovery, to make sure you stay on track, to ensure you're avoiding things that will trigger you. Like I said, devil's advocate."

"And what if I don't?"

His eyes stay locked on me as he chews and eventually swallows. "What if you don't what?"

"Walk away."

Dale considers me for a moment. "Then you're making it a thousand times harder on yourself to stay sober and clean. You're setting yourself up to fall and to fail. You know I will always be here for you, no matter what, but you have to understand the position you're putting yourself in every time you see that woman."

I lean back in the booth and stare at the one that Ivy and I sat in that day. "Well, luckily, I don't see her that much."

"Oh, that's right." His eyes widen. "You just sneak into her house while she's gone and drop things off and then sneak back out."

I smirk at him. "Pretty much."

"You know what that makes you?"

"If you say stalker..."

He barks out a laugh. "No, that's what you were before. Now? I don't know what the fuck you are. Maybe an altruistic lurker..." He motions toward my plate. "Eat. You need to. You look like you haven't been."

I clear my throat. "I am."

But he's right; my appetite seems to have fled the same way Ivy's did when Drew died. Though apparently, she had a very legitimate excuse for that, whereas for me, it's these welling emotions that always seem to clog my throat.

"Have you been painting at all?"

I glance up at him as I force myself to snag the silverware and cut into my plate. "No. Things are still too..." I shrug. "Mixed up. In a way that I can't quite break through."

"It was beautiful."

"What was?"

His gaze softens. "The one you did at Max's."

The corners of my lips curl. "You saw that, huh?"

He nods. "Would have been hard to miss it when it was all over the local news channels and the internet. I think you're moving in the right direction with that."

"What do you mean?"

Dale offers a shrug. "Concentrating on the happy memories, on the things that make you smile. It seems that you and Ivy are both so bogged down in your grief, in your anger, that you're clinging to it instead of letting it go and looking to the future."

He isn't wrong.

But what kind of future will it be if I have to walk away from Ivy and that baby?

The thought of it makes my stomach twist, and I drop my silverware onto the plate with a clatter and bury my face into my hands again.

Talking to Dale usually helps me sort through all the fog in my head, silences those voices and the little devil on my shoulder whispering for me to do stupid things. And today, he was the voice of reason.

But what if I don't want to listen to reason?

What if reason is what will truly decimate my heart?

21

CAM

FIVE DAYS LATER

PLEASE.

Six letters.

One simple word that says a thousand.

How long did it take her to get the nerve to send the text?

Minutes...

Hours...

Days...

How long has she sat there, staring at the screen, finger hovering over the send button?

It's been a week since I made that promise to her again.

A week since I saw her.

Since I touched her.

Since I *tasted* her.

And every moment since then, I haven't been able to stop thinking about it.

The look in her eyes when she asked me to do it. The plea in her voice. The way her body trembled under my touch and how she came apart on my tongue. The wash of her release coating my mouth and filling me with an ecstasy I had no right to feel.

I've obsessed over what happened with her, and after my talk with Dale, I've put all that angst and uncertainty onto the canvases that now line the walls of the studio.

Images that depict not just her pain—that I was so adamant I didn't want to show—but the raw beauty I saw in it and in her as she fought to stay above water and avoid drowning in her misery. As she asked for my help and accepted it.

Has she been thinking about it this entire time?

Considering taking me up on my offer?

How many times did she press the keys, then delete, only to retype it again?

Likely as many as I've started the car and thrown it into drive to head back home tonight, only to lose the nerve, put it in park, and shut it off again just to sit and stare at her house.

I move my hand to the ignition button to start the car, to do what I *should* have that night. When she opened that door and I stood there in the rain, in the gloom of the storm that had surrounded the house without that damn porch light, I should have walked away.

But as soon as I saw her face...the moment I witnessed how the same dark cloud that consumed me was swallowing her whole, I couldn't leave.

I couldn't let her wither and die with him.

That same need to save her, to offer her *anything* that

might keep her afloat in the raging tempest I have made her reality finally forces me to ignore Dale's warnings.

To pull my hand back from the ignition.

To open the door.

To take that first step across the pavement toward the house.

It is what pushes me up the front walk and to the porch and makes me knock.

I can't use my key tonight.

I can't just let myself in like I have so many other times.

Not for *this*.

Ivy doesn't answer, and maybe it's a sign I should turn around and go. But my phone dings, and I pull it out of my pocket and find a message from her.

Come in

Those two little words, coupled with the one she sent earlier, are enough to shatter any resolve I have left to walk away before this goes any further.

I made her a promise.

One I intend to fulfill.

My whole body vibrates in anticipation as I step inside, the thought of why she asked me to come over making every nerve in my body tingle while simultaneously causing my conscience to recoil.

Don't do this, Cam...

She may want it now, but she'll regret it later.

That little devil on my shoulder whispers louder the farther I move in, trying to drown out any thought about why this is so wrong and all those reasons Dale gave me only a handful of days ago.

Give her what you both want...

I shake my head, trying to stop the warring voices, but they're both still there as I make my way back to the bedroom.

Their bedroom.

Their bed.

So many things I swore would never happen, that I fought so hard to keep from coming to fruition, have slowly occurred over time. Promises to myself broken due to my own weaknesses and failures and through Ivy's persistent presence in my head.

Before I step in, I take a fortifying breath, but all that does is drag her scent into my lungs, making my cock stir to life before I've even *seen* her.

Get your shit together.

I'm not sure which voice is saying that—the one that wants me to leave or the one that wants me to fulfill my promise to her.

A promise I never should have made, because giving her what she wants now will only grow into something more complicated later, and we both know it.

This cosmic pull that seems intent on bringing us together over and over again doesn't seem to care about the fallout.

And right now, neither does Ivy.

Maybe I don't, either.

I make it to the door and find her lying on the bed, facing me.

She doesn't say a word, just watches me as I step in

and cautiously approach. Her gaze rakes over me—hot, needy, begging without saying a word for the very thing I swore I would give her if she ever asked.

Relief.

From all the turmoil I've brought into her life.

From all the agony she's suffering.

I'm the last person who should be giving it to her. The last person who has any right to touch her and love her the way she's asking, but I also can't say no to this woman.

Not when I see her in distress.

Not when there's something I can do about it.

I stop at the edge of the bed, my knees bumping against the mattress, and her eyes sweep up to meet mine. She holds out a hand to me silently, and I look at it for a moment.

Her delicate, slender fingers with short nails that won't get in the way of her work, digging around in the dirt and caring for all the plants at her shop. They look so soft reaching out for me, something that could never cause pain, that will only bring comfort and pleasure.

The way they curl slightly in offering, asking me to join her without a word, is enough to end that battle in my head.

Fuck...

I slide my palm along hers, clasping it firmly as I climb onto the bed, my knees sinking into the mattress as she rolls onto her back, tugging me with her. Her hand tightens around mine as I settle in next to her on my side, bracing myself up on my elbow. She loops our fingers together, dragging my arm across her expanding belly until I'm draped over her, gazing down at the face I've painted countless times.

Drinking her in.

Examining every feature that I know so well, that I dream about every night and fantasize about every day, to ensure she knows what she's doing and what she's asking for.

And her eyes are clear tonight.

No darkness rimming them that would reveal her tears.

No hesitation in the way they meet mine.

Her lips part subtly, a little breath floating out that doesn't sound at all concerned about the fact that she called me over here to get her off when we both know I should stay far away.

I run my fingers through her thick, dark hair. So soft. Smelling of honeysuckle and hope, a combination that always completely undoes me.

She holds my gaze for a few moments in the dark, but even without the lights on and only a thin sliver of moonlight filtering in from the window, it's clear there isn't any reservation there.

Just a burning need I've seen before.

Including that night that changed everything.

Ivy lured me in then with her sweetness, her innocence, her pure light that seemed to radiate from her across the yard, through the swaying branches of that willow tree. And once I spoke with her, once I saw her smile and heard that voice, I knew there was no hope for me to walk away that night.

There isn't now, either.

And she sees it.

Ivy lifts herself slightly to capture my mouth with hers.

The simple press of her lips after all this time ignites a fire deep inside me. One I've tried so hard to put out over the last four years. That burning need for her, the bone-deep, searing desire to give this woman anything and everything, to possess her, to consume her the way flames do everything in their path, to make her come apart in my arms and on my cock.

And that voice that only moments ago was telling me I shouldn't be doing this, that warned me that this is just another step back in my recovery by giving in to my addiction to her, that screams at me that she's the worst kind of drug a man like me could ever get a taste of, it silences as her tongue sweeps along mine and I get my taste of her.

She presses her hand to my chest, directly over my rapidly beating heart, her fingers clenching the fabric tightly.

I groan against her lips, and she issues a little needy moan, trying to press closer, but her growing belly prevents her from getting me where she wants me. A whimper of frustration falls from her mouth into mine, but it acts as a momentary reminder that what we're doing isn't good for either of us.

Ivy is using me to ease her pain.

I'm using her to fuel my addiction.

I tear my mouth from hers, searching her face for any reservation that could end this right now. "Are you sure this is what you want, Ivy?"

Because one word is all it would take to stop this. To

end this madness. To give us time to come to our senses instead of giving in to something that has only ever led to misery.

But instead of offering me that word, she nods, a frantic pant slipping from her lips. "Yes..."

That's probably her hormones talking.

Everything I've read in the pregnancy and baby books I've spent hours going through since I found out about this baby tells me some women get incredibly *hot* during certain parts of their pregnancies.

It would certainly explain how easily she's overlooking how much she hates me in order to get *this*.

It would explain why she can look at me and not just see the man who stole Drew from her.

But that doesn't mean I won't give it to her.

She might want this, might need it, in the moment, but I know she'll regret it in the morning.

She'll regret that she gave in to the hormones and the loneliness.

She'll regret that she let me touch her like this.

She'll regret the emotional fallout, just like I imagine she did last week when I walked out of here and left her in the shower.

There's nothing I can do about that.

There's nothing I can do to change how things worked out between us.

But at least I can give her a few hours away from those thoughts that plague her, from the agony that consumes her—and *me*.

Her fingers slide from my chest down to the hem of my T-shirt, frantically tugging at the fabric. I grasp it quickly and yank it over my head, letting it fall to the floor beside the bed. The cool air in the bedroom hits my hot skin, but the press of her palm against me sends a rush of heat through my body and straight to my straining cock.

I graze my lips along her collarbone, up her neck, and dip my head close to her ear as I reach between us to tug up her tank top. "Do you want me to fuck you, Ivy?"

She whimpers and nods, trying to shift closer as I trail my fingers across the sensitive skin under her breasts. Goosebumps break out over her flesh under my touch, and her nipples pebble.

My mouth waters at the sight of them, and I shift my head to suck one between my lips greedily.

Ivy arches into me, her nails scoring my chest.

I growl at the soft bite of pain, and my cock twitches behind the zipper of my jeans as I shift one leg until my thigh is settled between hers.

She moans, rolling her hips and grinding down, seeking that little bit of friction that only this angle will give her. The heat of her cunt through the thin fabric that covers it seeps through the denim into my thigh, and I drag my teeth across her nipple.

Her lips part. "Fuck!"

Ivy arches up and up, her back bowing, her body trembling until I release it with a soft pop. She gasps and sags onto the bed, her eyes hooded, stormy under thick, heavy lashes as she stares at me expectantly.

With her tank top bunched up above her breasts and only a tiny pair of sleep shorts barely covering her cunt, spread out across the bed, her dark hair splayed across the pale pillowcase like a halo, I could spend *days* memorizing every detail. Every shadow. Every dip and curve.

But I need to taste her.

I twist onto my back and drag her up across me until she straddles my waist. Her lush thighs tighten around me as she shifts, and I trail my hands along the waistband of her shorts.

She shivers, pressing her hands into my chest, fingertips curling as if begging me to continue. I slip them over her hips and down her thighs, and she pushes up onto her knees, pulling one leg, then the other, free, leaving her in only a thin thong that barely conceals her pussy.

Eyes locked with hers, I reach between her legs and glide my finger along the damp fabric.

A groan tumbles from her mouth, and she clenches her thighs around my hand, thrusting herself down slightly onto it.

"You're so wet already, Ivy. Were you thinking about me all night?"

She bites her bottom lip but nods, and the knowledge that she's been fantasizing about me, has been thinking about this as much as I have been, only spurs me on and helps wash away those last bits of reservation that lingered.

I drag the material to the side so I can touch her wet flesh, and she bucks in my hold.

My fingers glide easily through her slick slit.

She's more than ready.

Desperate in the same way that I am for her.

I grasp the edges of her thong, easily tearing the fabric, fully baring her to me.

And Christ, she's beautiful like this.

Wanton.

Needy.

Ready.

She rests a hand protectively over her stomach and watches me cautiously, almost as if she is afraid I don't like what I see, but I grasp her wrist and pull her hand out of the way, so I can slide my palms across her smooth skin.

A shiver rolls through her, and her eyes drift closed as her lip disappears under her teeth again.

"You're so fucking beautiful, Ivy." My voice cracks on her name. Because I shouldn't even be saying it. I shouldn't be here. I shouldn't be the one seeing her like this. I shouldn't be the one telling her this and reassuring her that she's never been sexier. "I have to taste you."

Her eyes fly open and meet mine, and I slide my hands around her waist and tug her up.

"Sit on my face, Ivy."

"What?"

Her lip quivers as she stares down at me, but I urge her up higher and higher until she's kneeling directly over my mouth, and her glistening pussy sits ready for me, only a few inches away.

"This is what I dream about. You. Like this. Getting to touch you." I glide my palms up the insides of her thighs, making her shudder. "And getting to do this."

I lift my head to drag my tongue through her.

She groans, the headboard creaking as she grips it above me to steady herself. Her knees tremble against my shoulders, and I lick along her seam, savoring her taste but somehow needing more.

Because I *need* her release.

I need to see and feel her come apart.

I need to know I've done that for her.

She grinds down on my mouth.

Seeking the same thing I am.

I growl my agreement, glide my hand up her leg, and thrust two fingers into her as I suck her clit between my lips. Her head falls back, and she moans, her body telling me exactly what she needs.

The contraction of her cunt around me.

The roll of her hips against my face.

The way her thighs tremble.

I devour her, showing her the only way I can think of how sorry I am for everything and how willing I am to do everything she asks.

For as long as she'll let me.

I suck her clit between my teeth and graze them along it, and she bucks so hard the headboard slams to the wall.

Yes.

That's what I want.

Ivy released from all the things holding her back—the pain and fear and loneliness—that keep her locked away in this room rather than out there living...

I repeat it, over and over again, alternating between light scrapes of my teeth along her wet flesh, flicks of my tongue, and thrusting my fingers deep inside her until her entire body undulates and she rides my face, taking what she wants, and accepting everything I have to give her in this moment.

It isn't nearly enough, not what she deserves, but when she finally comes on a silent gasp, the clasp of her pussy around my fingers, and the way she presses down on me somehow gives me the tiniest bit of relief, too.

Her body spasms as I continue to drag her orgasm out with each thrust and flick. And when I suck her clit into my mouth and bite down, a second wave hits her hard enough that she arches back and the headboard slams violently against the wall again before she sags forward.

I wrap my arms around her and help guide her down my body, until her belly presses into mine, and I can feel her heart beating in time with my own.

She shifts slightly, until her pussy settles over my hard cock still encased in my jeans. A strangled groan catches in my throat, but I force myself to swallow it, my fingers digging into her hips to still her movements.

I can't take it that far, no matter how badly I may want to.

And God knows I *want* to.

The thought of being like this with Ivy has been the only thing I've wanted for so long that I can't remember a time when I wanted anything else.

But not like this.

She lifts her head slowly, her eyes half-lidded and still fogged with her orgasm, and she rolls her hips, making it very clear what she wants. "Please, Cam. I just need—"

I press my thumb to her lips, silencing her. "I know, Ivy." I grit my teeth, shaking my head. Biting back the rush of words and explanations that want to come out. "But I can't. I just...I can't."

A tear trickles down her cheek as she shifts against me. "Please..."

Hell.

I did love to hear her beg. Those few days we spent together before everything imploded, I *lived* to know it was what she wanted.

But this is different.

So full of desperation that it's like that first night after we spread Drew's ashes. The first time I touched her after I had *sworn* to myself that I wouldn't ever again.

And it never should have happened.

Just like this shouldn't.

I capture her face between my palms and brush my lips over hers to soften the blow of my rejection. "You know I would do anything for you, Ivy—"

She presses her forehead to mine, her breath uneven, and a tear falls to my chest. "Then please give me this. I promise I'll hate you tomorrow."

22

CAM

Her words should give me pause.

They should make me stop this madness that already seems to have engulfed us.

Because I know she means them.

I know that deep down, she will never stop hating me and won't ever be able to forgive me for any of this—just like I know I won't ever be able to forgive myself.

But if anything, her promise does the opposite.

Almost as if it gives me permission to do the one thing I swore I wouldn't, the very thing Dale warned me would happen if I continued to place myself in her orbit.

My cock throbs where it's pinned beneath her wet core, and my hands flex into her lush thighs. Heat licks across every inch of me, tightening my skin until it feels like it might burst open. The tension permeating my body makes me tremble beneath her, and she pulls her head back and looks at me, the plea written there in her gaze.

Let her hate you tomorrow.

She needs you to love her tonight.

No matter what happened between us in the past, no matter what I may have done and how I may have hurt her, no matter how bad this might be for *me* in the end, this is what *she* needs, and with her looking at me like this—like she absolutely does *not* hate me—it's impossible for me to say no even if it might be the right thing to do.

And I can deal with the fallout later.

Not in this moment.

That's a problem for tomorrow.

Tonight is about Ivy and giving her *everything* that's in my power to give.

That simple realization is all it takes for me to crush my lips to hers, devouring her mouth the same way I just did her pussy. She whimpers and clutches my shoulders, her tongue gliding along mine, undoubtedly tasting her own release as she demands all the things I was so reluctant to give her.

Not because I don't want it.

Never that.

But because I don't *deserve* her or this.

I never did.

Ivy knows that as well as I do, but she's lost in the throes of her need, rolling against me as her hands slip to my waistband, fumbling at my button and zipper until she drags it down and is able to get inside.

The minute her smooth, warm palm hits my cock, I choke on my breath, my whole body bowing up toward her, a strangled gasp falling from my lips.

Fuuuuuck.

One simple touch from this woman and I'm falling apart, ready to come in her hand in an instant.

And it isn't just because I haven't had that kind of release since she last gave it to me months ago...

It's because this is what I've dreamed about, what I wanted. Not my own touch. Not fantasies and memories.

Her.

I wanted Ivy's soft but determined touch. Her fingers gripping my cock and stroking it in the way only she can. I needed her warm, panted breaths fluttering over my skin as she moves the pad of her thumb across the bead of pre-cum seeping from the head of my throbbing dick.

This is what I wanted, what I waited for, what I prayed would come, even as I knew asking for it made me the selfish bastard I have been trying to bury.

She shoves at the denim, trying to get it down to give herself better access, but her current position prevents her from moving it any farther. A frustrated sound falls from her lips before she rolls to the side, settling onto the bed to give me room to do it myself.

I push my jeans down, tug them off, and turn to toss them to the floor, but as I start to twist back toward her, something hot and wet engulfs my cock.

"Fuck..."

Gritting my teeth, I drop onto the mattress and find her head dipped over me, her mouth wrapped so tightly around me that I might instantly explode.

Jesus. Fucking. Christ.

I tunnel my fingers into her thick hair, gripping it tightly, and jerk her away. She releases my slick length, confusion narrowing her eyes as they meet mine.

Her wet lips glisten, so fucking inviting, and my cock aches to be back in that heat even as the tightening in my chest reminds me why I'm here—for *her*, not *me*. "As much as I've fantasized about coming down your throat, Ivy, I don't think that's what you really want tonight."

She whimpers, and I tighten my grip on her hair, angling her head down toward me, trying to get her to focus on why she asked me to come here tonight.

And it isn't for *this*.

This isn't why I'm here, either.

I feather my lips across her trembling ones. "Is it, Ivy?" Another sweep of them over her cheek. "Do you want my cock in your mouth tonight? Or do you want it somewhere else?"

She shudders against me, shifting closer.

It takes a second for her eyes to clear, for her to really *look* at me, and she finally shakes her head as much as she can with my hand buried in her dark tresses.

Good...

I release my hold on her hair, allowing her to move up onto her knees and straddle my thighs. Her slick core drags along my length, coating it thoroughly and drawing my balls up tight in my battle to hold back my release. One I am very close to losing thanks to Ivy.

I hiss at the contact as she continues to glide along me, grinding her clit as she presses her hands onto my chest, her short nails sinking into my skin with little sharp bites of pain.

Resting my hands on her hips, I dig my fingers in, stilling her movements long enough to say the words she needs to hear. "Take me, Ivy. Take whatever the fuck you need." Her eyes flutter open and meet mine. "I'm *yours*."

And I always have been, since that first moment I saw her.

She considers me for a second, looking down like she's seeing me for the first time, and a tear slips from her eye. Her fingers trail up from my chest and over my lips. I nip at them, then draw one into my mouth and suck on it the same way she just did my cock.

Her body twitches again, her hips rocking.

Whatever gave her pause vanishes as quickly as it came, and she pulls her hand from my face and grasps my cock, aligning it to her wet heat.

With her gaze locked on mine, she sinks down.

Fuuuuuccccckkkk.

Her hot, slick core engulfs me, and my eyes drift closed, my neck arching back at the feeling of being completely consumed by this woman. She gasps as I stretch her wide, and when she finally sinks down to the hilt, she crushes her clit against my pelvis.

Good God...

Pleasure courses through me, searing every nerve ending, consuming each minute fiber of my being, and washing away all those lingering doubts that this is the right thing, that *she* is the right thing.

I thought I had prepared myself for this.

The past week, I've thought about this moment and what I would do if she ever actually took me up on my offer, but I never imagined it could feel like this.

Like coming *home*.

Like being *complete* in a way I didn't think I could ever experience again.

It steals my breath, my words, my ability to do anything but live in this moment and the hot clasp of her heat.

She leans forward slightly, her belly pressing into mine, and I open my eyes to search hers for any sign that this is too much for her.

I lift one hand from her hip to take her cheek in my palm, brushing my thumb across it. "Are you okay?"

The books have told me enough to know that sex while pregnant is safe, but the fear of hurting her or the baby still freezes me in place, torn between giving her what I know she likes and holding back because of her condition.

Ivy never liked it slow and gentle.

She never wanted that from me.

And I have always been too out of control when it comes to her to argue otherwise.

But I would never do a single thing to this woman that might hurt her or this baby—even if that means walking away right now.

Her hooded eyes lift to meet my gaze, and she nods, a long rush of hot breath floating from her parted lips, then slowly lifts herself just to sink down at the same agonizingly languid pace.

She drops her head back, hair cascading behind her as she starts to ride me, raising herself on trembling thighs only to engulf my cock again with a tight squeeze each time she descends.

Each movement is so careful.

So measured.

So unlike how Ivy typically wants it.

I slide my hands down to her ass and help her, lifting her higher and faster, allowing her to slam down on me with even more force. She leans forward slightly, altering the angle enough to allow the head of my cock to catch inside her, and a gasp falls from her lips.

And they're too tempting.

Too fucking addicting to ignore.

I push myself up as far as I can get with her stomach between us and capture her mouth, swallowing down those little noises she makes as I brace my feet and thrust up into her.

Over and over again.

My cock drags along that perfect spot.

But I can tell it isn't enough.

I kiss her deeply, gliding my tongue along hers, slowing the intensity while grinding up with every thrust to ensure she's getting the most penetration and full contact.

Her legs tremble.

Her pussy clasps and pulses around me, seeking more.

Demanding it the same way I am each and every breath that falls from her mouth into mine.

She whimpers against my lips, and I squeeze her ass with my hand still there and tighten my grip on her cheek with the other, trying to hold her steady, to get her there. But I can feel her building frustration, despite how incredible this feels for both of us.

It isn't enough.

My cock may be ready to fucking explode deep in her cunt, but Ivy needs something *more.*

I tear my mouth from hers, tilting her face until her hazy gaze meets mine. "Do you need it harder, Ivy?"

"I need..." She shakes her head, her eyes closing tightly as her hips continue to move with mine. "I need..."

She can't get the words out, but I don't need her to.

Rolling us carefully to the side, I pull out and shift behind her up onto my knees. The mattress dips beneath my weight, and I slide my hands under her hips, helping her slide up onto her forearms so she's in the perfect position for me to thrust into her. My cock bottoms out inside her, so fucking deep and tight it feels like a vise constricting around it.

"Fucking hell, Ivy..."

She groans, rocking and adjusting her hips slightly until the head of my dick catches with my retreat. I grit my teeth, the heat at the base of my spine exploding out and threatening to undo all my willpower. But I refuse to give in to my own pleasure. I refuse to accept it when I'm here for *her.*

Instead, I plunge back into her again, sliding one hand around to cup her stomach. My fingers reverently stroke the expanding skin as I pump up into her, and she clutches the sheets in her hands, pressing her cheek into the mattress as silent cries fall from her parted lips.

If her hips weren't rolling so hard to meet each drive of mine, I'd be worried I'm hurting her, but she moves faster, slamming against me harder and harder as she chases her release.

But something is holding her back.

Whether it's conscious or not, her body is ready, but *something* is preventing her from letting go of all the coiled tension.

My hand drifts lower until I find her clit, and I glide my fingers across it rapidly as I kiss my way to her ear and suck the lobe between my teeth, grazing it gently. "Just remember you hate me, Ivy. Fuck me like you hate me, if that's what you need."

She shakes her head and whimpers, biting her bottom lip so hard I worry her teeth might break through it as she rolls her hips harder, thrusting back to meet every drive up of my hips.

A sob finally tears out of her, muffled against the bed but still ringing in my ears. "I do hate you…"

I plunge into her, stealing her breath for a moment, but as I withdraw, she shakes her head again, tears sliding down her face.

"I fucking hate you for how much you made me care about you. For how much you made me trust you. For how much you made me *need* you. I. Fucking. Hate. You. Camden. Usher."

Those words are the dam breaking—for both of us.

Just different kinds.

She comes on a silent gasp, her body jerking in my hold as I continue to drive into her, holding her tightly to me, twisting and rolling my fingers across her clit to drag it out until she finally comes down to earth.

And I'm still rock-hard embedded inside her.

Unable to come.

Unable to find what she did when what she said rings in my ears, and I hear the truth of every syllable.

She sags and rolls onto her side, my cock sliding from inside her. Heavy breaths slip from her parted lips. Her chest heaves, and half-lidded eyes watch me with such a confusing mix of emotions.

All I know is I have to go.

I climb off the bed and grab my jeans, tugging them on and tucking my slick, still-hard cock into them. Her unsure gaze follows my every move, but it's the combination of hatred and lust in her eyes that can't be separated that ultimately prevents me from saying anything.

Because there isn't anything left *to* say.

Even if I wanted to, I couldn't right now.

I grab the rest of my clothes and walk out without looking back because if I do, she will see the tears streaming down my cheeks, and she will know just how much hearing her say that broke me.

23

IVY

ONE MONTH LATER

Marlo pulls her car into the driveway and throws it into park, and I stare at the house that already feels so empty even before I've set foot back into it.

My chest tightens at the thought of going in there to be alone again after spending the weekend with her.

Mostly because I know it won't take very long before temptation comes calling again.

To text him.

To send that single little word, the only one I've been able to use when it comes to asking for what I want— *PLEASE.*

How can something so simple as that word be so complicated?

Because we've made it that way.

Because *I* have.

By repeatedly asking him to come fulfill my *needs* and take my pleasure while he never does himself, when I can

see what it's doing to him to keep sliding into my bed—
and me—only to walk away with a hard cock and barely
restrained tears shimmering in his eyes.

Yet, I can't stop asking him to come.

I can't stop *wanting* him here.

"Thanks again for coming with me."

Shit.

I drag my gaze from the house and glance at Marlo,
hoping she didn't notice how zoned out I just was. "No,
thanks for inviting me. Really, I needed this."

When she first suggested heading to New York for a
long weekend to see a Broadway show, have some great
food, and sight-see, I hadn't exactly been on board for a
multitude of reasons. Not the least of which was the
thought of going somewhere like that to pretend my life
hasn't fallen apart seemed wrong. And I hadn't believed
for a moment that I would be able to forget everything
that has happened—especially recently with Cam—and
actually enjoy myself.

But she had *insisted.*

And when Marlo sets her mind to something, she
usually gets it.

She wore me down with promises of delicious pizza,
Wicked, and shopping for things for the baby we would
never be able to find here in Philly.

It was that last item that really hit me square in the
chest and pushed me over the edge of accepting her invitation—because I haven't been able to bring myself to
begin even thinking about all the things I need to do for
this baby's arrival.

Our daughter will be here soon...

Sooner than I am ready for.

Because every time I open a website to start shopping for all the things I'll need to convert the guest room into a nursery and all the items necessary to actually take care of a newborn, I get so overwhelmed that I feel like I can't breathe.

And I can't tell Nancy.

She'll think I'm not happy about this baby, that I don't see her for what she is—a *miracle*. A tiny piece of Drew and a reminder of our love that will be with me forever. And I can't ever let her think that.

So, I went to New York, and somehow, little by little, the longer we were there, the easier it became to pretend I wasn't coming back to this cold, empty house and for me to actually start buying things for the baby—even if it was only a handful of outfits from some fancy boutique.

But I can't ignore what's waiting for me inside anymore.

Not when it's right in front of me and I have nowhere else to go.

Marlo smiles at me. "We need to do more girls' weekends." Her eyebrows waggle suggestively. "That guy I met on Friday night was hot as fuck."

I snort as I reach down to grab my purse, shifting awkwardly around my stomach to get it off the floorboard. "I'm glad you had a good time."

And I assume she *did,* since she didn't come back to our room until after two am.

My eyes drift to the dark windows again, and I pull my lip between my teeth. "Do you...want to come in for a while? We could order dinner."

She glances at the house and shakes her head. "No, I need to get home. Go to bed early. I have this real hard-ass boss who wants me at work at 6 am tomorrow."

Rolling my eyes and fighting a grin, I grasp the door handle. "Ha fucking ha."

I push open my door, and she climbs out, pulls my small roller bag from the trunk, and walks me to the porch.

The porch light shines above me.

Did I leave that on all weekend?

My mind has felt like Swiss cheese lately, thanks to the same hormones that are making me text Cam to come over at least once a week, so I don't remember if I did or not.

I must have...

Maybe believing it would ensure anyone driving by would think someone was home.

I turn the key in the lock and nudge the door open, and Marlo passes me the handle on my bag.

"I'll see you in the morning." She gives the house one last look, and something I can't quite place dances across her eyes—excitement maybe, though what could be so interesting that she has to rush home for it is beyond me. "Have a good night. I'll see you tomorrow."

She hustles to the car and backs out of the driveway, honking a few times before she drives off down the street. Despite the bite of winter air, I watch until she disappears around the corner before I step into the house with my bag and throw the lock behind me.

What the...?

Something's off.

I'm used to coming home to Cam's scent, left when he delivers dinners, healthy snacks, and whatever fruit the baby is the size of each week before heading to his meetings.

But this is different.

It doesn't just smell like Cam—that leather and citrus scent that used to soothe me but now causes a whirlwind of emotions to turn inside me. This smells like his *studio*.

Setting my purse on the kitchen counter, I scan for any signs that he's been here and find a note sitting beside a spaghetti squash.

The baby is the size of a spaghetti squash at 26 weeks.

Another note sits below it, as if he came back later and decided to add to the message.

If you don't like it, I can change it.

Don't like what?

The living room and kitchen appear untouched since I left on Thursday with Marlo, but I know he's been here as surely as I know that whatever he did will likely throw a new emotional curveball at me I'm wholly unprepared for.

Because that's what Cam does.

What he's *best* at.

He works his way under my skin.

Through sweet gestures...

And warm, strong hands that hold me when all I want is to fall apart.

My body trembles now, anticipating what I might find, and my hands wrap protectively around my belly as I make my way past the office door, my bedroom, and toward the cracked one at the end of the hallway—the guest room.

Light streams out of it, and I know I didn't leave that on.

There hasn't been any reason for me to go into that room for months, when I couldn't even bring myself to consider what needed to go into it for the baby.

My footsteps slow as I get closer, and the smell of paint grows heavier.

I nudge the door open hesitantly...

And my breath catches.

The sound of a key in the front door should drag my attention away from the room, but I'm frozen in place, my heart in my throat.

Familiar, booted footsteps approach from behind me, and then his scent envelops me, quickly followed by the heat of his body so close I can feel it at my back.

But he doesn't touch me as I try to take in what lies in front of me.

What did he do?

24

CAM

Ivy stands frozen in front of me, just inside the doorjamb, staring into what was a guest room that held nothing more than a twin bed and a dresser. What she and Drew had once hoped would eventually become a nursery for their theoretical baby. The one they tried so hard for and thought wasn't going to happen...

It became an empty tomb, a place Ivy never went, the same way she wouldn't have entered Drew's office if I hadn't wanted to go through those boxes.

But it isn't that anymore.

At least, I hope she won't see it that way.

Her eyes move across the space, taking in every detail, but they keep returning to the far wall—to the thing I *knew* I had to do the more I thought about what Dale said to me.

It just took me a while to figure out that it's what I needed to do—for Ivy.

And for myself.

A step toward looking forward instead of back by concentrating on the moment we let Drew go, that we stopped clinging to him and set him free in the place he loved so much.

Her body starts trembling, and my stomach twists.

Shit.

Maybe I shouldn't have done this.

Maybe I got it all wrong.

I lean to the side slightly so I can see her face and try to gauge just how badly I fucked this up.

Tears well in her eyes, and she reaches a hand from where it rests on her belly up to swipe them away as she absorbs all the work I've done over the last several days.

The longer she remains silent, the more confident I become that I made a huge mistake in doing this.

I've overstepped.

Massively.

I've inserted myself into her life in a place and way she never wanted me.

And why would she?

This isn't my place.

It never will be.

My gaze drifts to her stomach, to the place I felt my niece kick for the first time. My hand tingles with the memory, wanting so badly to feel it again. "Ivy, I'm sorry. I can change it. I can paint over it tomorrow, and you won't ever have to see it again. I just thought—"

Her head finally turns, and her gaze meets mine.

But there isn't any anger or animosity in her eyes.

Always pain, but not that.

She gives me a half-smile that shatters me completely

because it might be the first real *hint* of joy I've seen from her since the night everything fell apart. "It's perfect."

Those two simple words immediately soothe some of the uncertainty and turmoil swirling inside me, but her tears haven't convinced me that I didn't mess up big time by doing this, especially without telling her first.

And she may not see what I chose for the theme of the nursery the way I do...

Ivy takes a hesitant step inside, and I follow her, giving her space, unsure if she even wants me in here with her—now or ever.

The mural I painstakingly painted takes up the entire far wall.

Strathmere Beach at night with the moon reflecting off the water, exactly how it looked the night we spread Drew's ashes...

Her gaze stays locked on it for several minutes, taking in every nuance—the dark blues, black, white, and grays necessary to truly capture the image.

"How'd you do it?" Her eyes flick over to me. "It looks exactly like that night."

Unease tingles my spine, and for some reason, I don't want to tell her even though there isn't any reason not to.

I clear my throat. "Uh, Roxy helped me with the color palette."

Because there's no way I could have done *this* version of it on my own.

It would have been a colorless representation of what *I* saw, but not what *she* did. And not how their baby should see that beach or that night.

She flinches slightly, as if the mere mention of another

woman is enough to hurt her, but then she smiles. "It's beautiful."

I step in farther and stand near the crib that sits between the new matching dresser and changing table, while the rocking chair occupies the corner closest to the mural, tucked in under the moon we stood beneath that night.

And seeing her stand there now, in front of it, it's almost like being back on that beach, with our feet sinking into that sand and our anguish threatening to drown us as we said our final goodbyes to him.

God, I hope I got it right...

All of it.

"You have to tell me if you don't like anything. I just thought..." I swallow thickly, my eyes drifting to the large heart-shaped vase that I painted Drew's name on sitting on top of the dresser filled with sand from Strathmere. My gaze ghosts over the paintings I did to decorate the walls featuring friendly, cartoonish sea creatures. "I just thought your daughter should have him with her all the time, and this is the closest I could get to giving that to her...and you."

A sob slips from Ivy's lips, and she slaps a hand over her mouth, the tears flowing freely down her cheeks.

Her eyes move across the room now, taking in all the minute details, and she slowly walks over and slides her hand across the glass vase holding the sand, her palm settling on Drew's name.

I don't have to tell her where it came from.

She knows.

Just like I knew I needed to do this for her. For *him*. And for their daughter.

Because Ivy hasn't done anything to get ready for the baby.

She hasn't been able to bring herself to even begin to look for anything for this room, let alone spend the time putting together furniture and decorating.

And I can't say I blame her for that.

These are the things she should be doing with Drew.

It should be a joyful time filled with looking forward to all the new firsts and the future ahead of them, but she doesn't have that. At least, not in the same way she would have if Drew were still here.

She's facing it with the cloud of what she lost darkening her joy, impeding her ability to tackle all the projects that need to happen before she gives birth.

So even if she hates it, I had to try.

To do *something.*

Like I need to now as this heavy silence fills the space between us.

I motion toward the air purifier in the corner. "That should take care of the remaining paint smell in the next day or two, but I made sure to use a kind that is safe to be around."

She nods, her hand still plastered over her mouth, then she makes her way to the crib, trailing her fingers along the wooden rail and staring down at the bedding Mom helped me pick out.

"My mom said the sea theme would be perfect."

Ivy's gaze lifts to mine, and she drops her hand, her

lips parted slightly. "Your mom knew you were doing this?"

I nod.

Her dark eyebrows fly up. "Did *Marlo*?"

Despite my best efforts, I can't fight the twitch of my lips. "It was a concerted effort to get you out of town for a few days."

Those tear-soaked eyes widen even more. "That little liar."

I shake my head. "Please don't be mad at her. When I told her what I wanted to do and how much time I would need, she assured me she would figure out a way to get you out of here long enough for me to complete it. And to make sure you had a good time." Though, that part Marlo seemed less confident about, considering the almost zombie-like state Ivy has seemed to exist in for the last couple of months. "How *was* New York?"

She rests her hands on the crib rail and stares at the mobile dangling above it with smiling crabs, lobsters, fish, sharks, and seahorses turning over where the baby will sleep. "It was good. I think getting away from here for a while was actually exactly what I needed."

What she needed?

The way she said those words is enough to make me suddenly dread the answer to my next question. "For what?"

Her eyes slowly lift to meet mine. "To get some perspective."

My chest tightens at the intensity of her gaze, and I lean back against the wall, fighting the urge to go to her and pull her into my arms. To plead my case when she finally admits we shouldn't be doing what we have been. When she ends the only reason I get to see her, get to touch her, get to spend *any* time with her, even if it hurts.

I watch her, waiting for her to expand, but she doesn't say anything else, just wanders over to the rocking chair and sits in it, resting her hands on her belly.

She pushes off with her feet and glides back and forth, a small smile spreading on her lips.

"Do you like it?"

I keep asking her that, like some broken record that should have been thrown out a long time ago, but each and every thing in here was selected for a reason, and if I got it wrong, I need to fix it.

Because there are so many other things I can't fix.

Things that will haunt me every day for the rest of my life.

The ones in this room are easy.

Those? Not so much.

"I love it. Really." She swallows hard, like she's struggling to keep her emotions in check as much as I am. "Please thank Roxy for me."

I nod slowly, watching the way she cradles her belly so protectively. "I will."

"Are you two...?"

The way she doesn't finish the question has me lifting my head and searching her face.

Is that a hint of jealousy, or is believing that just wishful thinking?

It's impossible to know where I stand with Ivy after everything that's happened.

We've spent months dancing around each other.

Pretending that falling into bed together whenever she asks me to come over, only to have me walk away with my heart in my throat, is somehow okay. Avoiding the reality of what we're doing to ourselves and each other each time I touch her. Denying the fact that she still hates and blames me, even as she seeks me out to find comfort with increasing frequency. Ignoring the fact that as much as she despises me and tells me as much as I give her physical pleasure, I still love her—more now than ever.

I offer a weighted sigh. "I sat down with her a while back and explained some stuff to her that she needed to know about my addiction and recovery. To understand what happened between us and why."

Ivy's gaze softens, the hand stroking her belly stilling. "And?"

"And she accepted my apology, even if she shouldn't have, even if I have a lot more amends to make." I shrug. "But we're good now. *Friends.*"

My emphasis on that final word may be a bit much, but I don't want Ivy thinking there's anything going on between Roxy and me. I care about her as one of my oldest friends, as someone I used to confide in and who has supported me through many years by keeping my identity secret, and that's it.

That's all it will ever be.

And now that we've cleared the air, we've managed to fall into how things were before so easily that working with her on this mural and the room felt like stepping back in time to before I fucked up everything.

Ivy nods, chewing on her bottom lip as she continues to rock. "Good. I'm glad you have a friend here in Philly."

I give her a tight smile. "Me, too."

Making amends with Roxy helped alleviate some of the guilt I felt about what happened between us, but there are so many other things that I can never make up for.

This room feels like a woefully inadequate step, but it is one nonetheless.

"My mom did some shopping for you..."

She raises a brow, and I motion toward the dresser and the closed closet doors. Her rocking stops, and she cautiously climbs to her feet, using the chair arm to brace herself.

The larger her belly grows, the more nervous I become about what will happen when this baby arrives.

Not because I doubt for one moment that Ivy loves her daughter with every fiber of her being, but mostly because I'm aware of how painful each little milestone will be for her. She has Marlo, Trina, and Mom to help her, to be at her side, to give her advice and assistance, yet I know she will constantly be thinking about Drew not being here.

It's a constant dark whirlpool that could drag her under if she's not aware of it—something I'm all too familiar with.

She reaches the closet and slides open the doors. Her breath catches as her eyes sweep over all the little dresses and other outfits hung neatly on the rail.

Her gaze shifts to the dresser, and she walks over and tugs it open, each drawer filled with more outfits, onesies, itty-bitty socks, and every other adorable piece of clothing a baby could ever want or need.

Ivy's hands tighten on the top of the drawer, and her head falls low, a sob ripping through her...

And I can't take it anymore.

I can't stand here and watch her like this.

Her pain calls to me like a beacon in a storm, even though I'm the one who brought this maelstrom down upon her in the first place.

I make my way over to her cautiously, stepping up behind her like I have so many other times, but this feels different somehow. Even more forbidden than what we did on that couch the night we spread Drew's ashes. Even more so than what we've been doing in *their* bed. Because we're in *here*.

A space that was built for *their* child.

I slide one arm across her chest and the other down low around her belly, tugging her back to me and holding her tightly.

The sobs continue to rack her body, making her tremble in my embrace, and being the sick fuck that I am, I bury my face in her hair.

"Please don't cry, Ivy. I hate to see you like this."

She shakes her head slightly, then slides her hand to twine her fingers with mine across her belly. "I know, but these are happy ones. Mostly."

I feather my lips against her temple. "Mostly?"

It takes her a few moments to answer when the only sounds in the room are her soft sniffles and the air purifier running.

Then she finally nods. "He would have loved this. All of it..."

I swallow through a tightness in my throat and clear it. "If he were here, he would have done a dinosaur theme."

She lets out a laugh that's half-humor and half-agony

and turns her head slightly to look back at me. "For a girl?"

I nod. "He was so obsessed with them when we were little, and he would argue that they're gender neutral."

The corners of her lips twitch. "Yeah, I guess they kind of are."

"You know, he wanted to be a paleontologist at one point..."

Her brows rise as her eyes widen. "Really?"

"I think he might have gone that direction if Mom had never gotten sick. He loved science and investigating things that weren't completely understood."

She nods. "I can see that."

I grin at her, happy to see some humor in her eyes and on her face, but the conversation only reiterates that this really wasn't my place. "Should I have done that? Because he would have wanted it that way?"

There isn't any playbook for where we find ourselves right now, and it feels like everything I do, every decision I make, might be the wrong one—this included.

Tears pooling in her eyes again, Ivy shakes her head. "No. This is...this is..." Her gaze shifts over to the mural again, and a smile pulls at her lips. "This is *right*."

Fuck.

She has no idea how badly I needed to hear that.

How I've spent the last several days agonizing over every single brush stroke, wondering if it was right...

How many times I stopped and broke down, dropping to the floor and sitting with my face in my hands, sobbing until I had no more tears left...

And now, I can finally take a deep breath again, knowing she loves it.

I squeeze her gently, and she reluctantly releases her fingers from mine, allowing me to slip away. Because I don't trust myself to be this close to her anymore. I never did, and now, more than ever, she needs her space, and I need to get my head on straight.

Clearing my throat, I run my hand through my hair and retreat toward the door. "I should get going."

She nods, watching me with a mix of longing and uncertainty swirling in her eyes. "Yeah, it's getting late..."

I pause inside the jamb, letting my gaze drift across the finished room and her standing in it, looking so fucking stunning that it takes my breath away. This is where she belongs. This is where she'll feed and rock the baby to sleep. This is where she'll tell her bedtime stories about fantastical creatures...and her father.

Drew's fiancée.

Drew's baby.

I have to keep reminding myself of that.

That she isn't mine, that the baby isn't...

But all I've been able to think about since the day I found out she was pregnant is how much I love both of them.

Even if she keeps hating me.

25

IVY

"Are you going to sit there moping all day?"

I scowl at Marlo and offer a slight shrug, shifting on the plastic chair that offers absolutely no comfort or support, especially in my current condition. It feels like this baby grew exponentially overnight, and my back agrees with that assessment, as do my swollen feet. "That's the plan."

She releases an annoyed huff and returns to sorting the flower shipment, preparing everything for the busy weekend to come, with two weddings, a bar mitzvah, and a quinceañera, all happening on Saturday. "Well, I could really use your help."

Pressing my lips together tightly, I glare at her. "And I really could have used a heads up about what I was walking into last night..."

Her hands still as her eyes narrow on me. "Are you seriously mad?"

Now it's my turn to release a heavy sigh.

I don't know if "mad" is the right word, but since Cam left last night I've spent hours sitting in that room, looking at everything he did for me, knowing that Marlo and Nancy planned all this behind my back, and even though I don't want it to, it somehow feels like the sting of betrayal—like it was a statement that they had no faith in me that I would eventually get my shit together to do it myself.

And knowing they thought I would ever fail my baby in that way hits even harder when I consider the fact that no one said anything to me about it. Almost as if they were afraid that bringing it up was going to send me into a worse place.

Don't they know how much I love this baby?

Tears sting my eyes despite my telling myself I *wouldn't* cry when I came into work this morning, knowing I would see Marlo and likely have this conversation. "How long were you talking to him about this and planning it?"

She brushes off her hands and releases a heavy sigh, then comes and sits on the edge of the table in front of me. "At the risk of pissing you off even more"—I brace myself for her response—"I've been talking to Cam a lot."

"You what?"

Something that feels an awful lot like jealousy crawls up my tight throat as I stare at my beautiful best friend.

With her bright smile.

Gorgeous blond hair that somehow manages to look sexy even when she pulls it back into a messy bun.

Bright green eyes that always seem so full of mischief and joy.

Who doesn't look and *feel* like a beached whale right now.

Marlo is every man's wet dream...

She narrows her eyes at me, annoyance tightening her mouth. "Not like that, and you know it, so stop looking at me that way. He's been worried about you. Rightfully so. And I've been worried about both of you, so I've been meeting with him, going to coffee, occasionally lunch on days I have off."

I play with the hem of my shirt, that feeling in my throat not easing, but I manage to swallow through it. "What do you two talk about?"

"What do you think?"

My cheeks heat. "Remember when you told me you were risking me getting madder?"

She throws up her hands. "Not like that, Ivy. We're not talking about you behind your back like some mean girls. We both love you, and we're worried. I've been your best friend for most of your goddamn life, and you've barely spoken to me about any of this since Cam came clean. All I know is that it seems like you're falling back into that place you were when Drew died, the place Cam somehow got you out of."

I cringe because she isn't wrong.

Things have been bad.

Most days, it feels like time isn't moving at all.

Some, I wouldn't even get out of bed if I wasn't so worried about the baby and ensuring I eat and drink and take my vitamins and do all the things the book I bought tells me I *should* be doing.

Marlo clears her throat. "Plus..."

I lift my head and meet her intense gaze.

"I know you've been sleeping with him again."

Shit.

I squeeze my eyes closed, but the memories assault me almost instantly—of his touch, his kiss, the way he seems to bring me back to life with every single thing he does...

And how he walks away after looking like I've destroyed him.

"I'm not judging you."

"Really?" I open my eyes and meet hers. "Because it sounds like you are."

She shakes her head. "I'm not. Things between you and Cam are..." A mirthless laugh slips from her lips. "Complicated doesn't even begin to cover it. And I know pregnancy hormones do"—she lays her hands over my stomach—"crazy things to people. I've read all about how insanely horny you can get."

I bury my face in my hands, my cheeks heating. "Jesus Christ..."

"What? That's what the article said. So, I don't blame you for seeking an outlet for that. One that you think is safe. But we both know with you and Cam, things are *not* safe because it's *not* just sex, and you both *know* that."

A frustrated groan rumbles in my chest because she's right.

Things will never be *just sex* with Cam.

They never could be, no matter how badly I want to make it be nothing. No matter how badly I want to keep feelings out of it and just take what he can give me and allow him to walk away as if it isn't hurting both of us. As if I don't lie awake for hours after he leaves, wondering if I should call him, forcing myself not to call him and beg him to come back...

"Do you remember that day we went and saw the mural?"

I lift my head and nod, finally looking at her again. "Yes."

Her gaze has softened. "Do you remember what you told me?"

The warmth that flooded my chest at seeing the painting of young Cam and Drew together, doing something that meant so much to them, and their short relationship with their father, comes back.

I nod. "Yes."

"Well, I'm going to remind you anyway. You told me that you didn't know what to do with all these feelings. That you didn't know what to do with him when you couldn't stop hating him and being so angry."

"I remember what I said."

"Good." She levels a hard gaze at me that demands I look deep into my soul when I answer whatever she's about to ask. "But is that how you *actually* feel? Is that how you felt that day? Is that how you feel now? Because the way I see things, what I've seen from you over the past several months during the very few times we've discussed Cam and what happened, does not look like hate, Ivy."

My eyes start to burn, my chest tightening as she stares me down with an accusation in her gaze. One I am wholly unprepared to face.

I shake my head. "Don't say it."

She tightens her jaw. "Not going to back down."

Because she never does.

"I know you don't want to hear it, Ivy, and I believe that saying it will probably piss you the fuck off even more, but you need to hear it. You're in *love* with Cam. You've been in love with Cam this entire time. What he did, what happened, hasn't changed that, and *that's* why it hurts so much. If you *actually* hated him, if you *actually* blamed him for everything and truly deep down believed that it was all his fault, this would be *easy*. You could walk away. You could end whatever this is with him instead of needing him as much as you do and doing backward somersaults trying to make excuses for why you're doing it."

I open my mouth to object, but she holds up a hand.

"No. You're going to *listen,* and *then* you can tell me off when I'm done."

I snort, fully prepared to do just that.

Because this version of Marlo is the scary one.

The one that usually makes *sense* when nothing and no one else does.

She somehow breaks things down to what lies at the core—that thing you *have* to see.

And it usually hurts.

"When Cam showed up, it was a jolt to your system, a shock to see someone who looked so much like Drew, who shared so many of the things with the man you loved so much, and you did your best to shut him out from your life. You were mad about their falling out, even before you knew what caused it, and you were holding it against him. That made it easy for you to keep him at arm's length, but the moment you started getting to know him? The moment he became more than just Drew's brother?" She shakes her head, offering a half-smile. "I saw you start to forgive him before you even knew what had caused their rift because he was *helping* you. You were coming back to life. You told me yourself that being with him made things easier, and that's clearly the case now, too, or you wouldn't keep going back to him. So, I don't understand why you keep lying to yourself about why any of this is happening. Why can't you just admit that you love him?"

I slap my hand over my mouth before the sob that crawls up my throat can rip out. The tears that well finally spill out, running hot down my cheeks, and I shake my head. "I can't be in love with him, Marlo. I just *can't*."

She holds my gaze, unwavering. "Why not?"

Why not?

What the hell kind of a question is that?

"Because. There's too much history. There's too much..." I throw my hands up because words escape me to describe everything that's been welling up inside me since Cam appeared on my doorstep. "This is *all* his fault, Marlo. *All* of it."

"Is it?"

The silence that fills the air after her simple question weighs down on me, threatening to crush my chest, and I protectively press my hands over my belly. "How can you even ask that?"

My voice wavers, but she doesn't bend.

She continues to stare me down with a brow raised. "Because I think you know as well as I do that it *isn't* his fault. What happened in the garden that night—yes, he lied to you. He pretended to be Drew, and that was a really fucking shitty thing to do, but Ivy? You knew something was different about him that night. That the person sitting with you on that bench was not the Drew that you had been dating, and you can't deny that. You've told me as much. You have wanted *Cam* since the moment you met him, plain and simple. And that doesn't take anything away from what you had with *Drew*. You two..." A little laugh falls from her lips, and she sighs. "God, it was disgusting how much in love you were, and I've never been more jealous of anything in my life than I was of your relationship."

I sniffle. "Really?"

Her head bobs.

"How come you never told me that?"

"Because I was also ludicrously happy for you. I've never seen you like that with anyone until Drew." She dips down slightly to catch my gaze. "And now, Cam. He *does* something to you, Ivy. I didn't think *anything* would pull you out of the depression you were in when you lost Drew—"

"I wasn't depressed."

She snorts and shakes her head. "Oh, honey. You were, most definitely, depressed. And Nancy, Trina, and I did everything we could think of to help you out of it, but you didn't *want* to come out of it. That *changed* when Cam showed up. When he started telling you those stories about Drew. When he cried with you. When he pushed you to let go of his ashes and attempt to find your way back to your life again."

I wince. "I can't love him."

I repeat the words I've already said as if saying them more will somehow make everything I'm feeling go away.

But I know they won't.

"You can."

My lip trembles as I fight another sob. "But *how*?"

"Because love isn't rational, Ivy." She sighs. "*You* don't control it; it controls *you*. And I've never seen a situation more fucked up than the one you're in right now, believe me, but it doesn't negate those feelings. It doesn't turn them off and make them go away. And it isn't instantly going to resolve just because you don't *want* to love Camden Usher. The truth of the matter is, you loved Drew. You still do."

Marlo slides off the table and squats in front of me, resting her hands on top of mine on my stomach.

"And you're about to have a beautiful daughter, and he would have loved her *very* much." Tears leak from my eyes as she stares at me. "But he's gone."

My chest tightens.

"And Cam is here. And Cam loves you. And he loves this baby. And he's her uncle. And he's not going *anywhere*. Not unless you explicitly tell him to, which I know you don't have the heart to do because you love him, too. You just have to accept that."

I shake my head, a sob catching in my throat again. "I can't."

"Maybe you can't right now, but eventually, you will, and he's still going to be here. But the longer you wait, the longer you don't talk about this and try to convince yourself that you hate his guts while you're still sleeping with him and letting him hold you at night, the harder you're making it on yourself and on him. And you're not a vindictive person, Ivy." She squeezes my hand. "I know you don't want to cause him any more pain than he's already suffered, either. Both of you have suffered enough for ten thousand lifetimes, and it's time for you both to let it go instead of clinging to it."

I wish I could so easily believe Marlo's words.

I wish it were that easy to forget everything that's happened and move on from it.

I wish I could just *let go* instead of clinging to what I have left of Drew.

I wish Cam Usher had never come home for his mom's birthday party that night.

I wish I had never seen him.

I wish I had never called out.

Because it's partially my fault, too.

26

CAM
ONE WEEK LATER

Quiet conversations float through the air as everyone takes their seats and settles in for the start of the meeting. I slide into my usual spot in the back row and pull off my leather jacket, draping it on the seat next to me and running a hand through my hair to push it off my face.

Though tonight, I feel more like hiding behind it.

Not a word from Ivy since last week when we spoke in the nursery.

No texts.

No calls.

Just an endless void in my chest.

I'm not sure what I expected after that night, but returning to slipping into her house like some deranged stalker while she's gone to leave her food and random fruits on the counter definitely wasn't it.

Nor was feeling like I had somehow done something

wrong when she insisted it was perfect and that she didn't want anything changed.

Each time it feels like there might be a tiny step forward with Ivy, I end up right back where I started—desperate for any way to help her.

And I feel like I'm failing over and over again.

So, tonight's meeting will be good.

I need to talk.

I've been coming here long enough that almost everyone knows what happened by now—at least those parts I've shared, which have given them the basics—and as much as I may not want to discuss all the things I've done wrong and ways I've hurt everyone around me, it *does* help.

Sometimes, it's the only thing that does.

It's better than sitting alone in my studio, staring at another canvas, struggling to find a way to express all this turmoil while that little voice tries to tell me there are ways to make it go away...

Dale approaches, inclining his head and giving me a look that says how shitty I feel is written all over my face. He settles to my left, leaning back in the metal chair and resting his arms across those on either side. "You good?"

It's the same question he always asks, and my answer has varied greatly the past several months. There have been nights when he's come to the studio and sat with me over a carafe of coffee because I didn't want to call Mom and couldn't be alone with the thoughts in my head. There have been breakfasts and lunches when I actually felt good and walked away thinking things were going to get better.

And in many ways, they have.

I'm in a much better place than I was that night I almost went back down that very dark path. Even with all the anguish and uncertainty revolving around Ivy, I can at least *breathe* again most days.

So, even though I may want to hide tonight and wallow, I refuse to give in to it.

Instead, I nod—despite the silence from Ivy weighing down on me like a thousand-pound elephant on my chest.

"You don't look okay." His assessing gaze rakes over me, and I know what he sees. My uncut hair that has grown completely out of control. My unshaven face. The bags under my eyes. My shaking hands that keep searching for something to do since the only paintings that have truly felt *right* recently have been the mural I did of Drew and me and the nursery. "Are you sleeping?"

I shake my head because there's no denying what must be written all over my face. "Not a lot."

The only time I seem to be able to close my eyes and actually find any sort of peace is when I'm with Ivy, and every time, I force myself to get up. To get dressed again. To leave her alone in Drew's bed and walk away.

Because it's just sex.

It's just giving her what she physically needs right now.

It's just being what I can for her in any way I can.

And I don't have a right to take anything for myself, even a few hours of contented sleep I so desperately need with her in my arms.

I've done that selfish thing before and look where it got all of us...

Dale opens his mouth to say something that would no doubt be wise and just as likely something I don't want to hear, but his eyes widen slightly at something behind me. "I...think you have a guest tonight."

Mom?

She has offered to come to meetings with me more times than I can count, and I've taken her up on it occasionally. But we talked earlier today, and she never mentioned it—

I turn, expecting to see her waiting.

But a different dark-haired woman fills my gaze instead, the one I've longed so hard to see that for a brief moment, I wonder if she's some sort of mirage.

Ivy stands inside the doors to the meeting room, bundled up in her peacoat that barely closes around her protruding belly, her eyes scanning nervously over the chairs. When they find me, her shoulders stiffen slightly, and she seems to suck in a sharp breath before she slowly walks forward.

Each step she moves closer, my heart beats faster until it's thundering against my ribs. All the air rushes from my lungs when she reaches me, all the words I've been wanting to say suddenly stuck in my throat.

I hear—rather than see—Dale get up and move out of his chair as she stares down at me, her soft brow furrowed.

She chews on her bottom lip, looking around again before returning her uncertain gaze to me. "Hi."

God, has it really only been a week since I've heard her voice?

It feels like an eternity since I held her in my arms in

the nursery, and the trepidation in her eyes now crushes me almost as much as that night did.

I swallow thickly, trying to work through the shock and emotion that want to choke me. "Umm, hi. Is everything okay?"

Because why else would she be here?

For her to show up, something serious must be happening.

My gut immediately tightens, dozens of different possible reasons she could be here flickering through my head, but she nods.

Her gaze cuts around the room again, and she shifts nervously. "Is it okay that I'm here?"

She came for the meeting?

It takes a second for my brain to process her question...and her intent to stay.

She came for you...

That realization is enough to make me want to drag her down into my arms and kiss her senseless, but I don't know what any of this means, and true fear of doing or saying something that might send her running keeps my hands clenched at my sides instead.

"Yeah. Uh, it's an open meeting, so...family and friends are welcome..."

I trail off because I don't know what Ivy is.

Not technically family; definitely not just a friend.

We're forever stuck in this weird place, a vicious cycle of pain and pleasure, hate and need, and it's reached the point that we're about to be completely destroyed by it.

She purses her lips, nervously shuffling her feet again,

and rubbing her hand across her stomach. "Is it okay with *you?*"

Fucking hell...

Tears threaten, already burning in my eyes, but I somehow manage to blink them back and nod as I pull my jacket from the seat closest to the aisle and move it to the one Dale just vacated on my other side, giving her room to sit.

She offers me a tentative smile and slides in, settling and adjusting herself as if she's uncomfortable—but whether it's with the shitty chairs or the fact that she's here at all remains as much of a mystery to me as what is going on inside her head.

Manny starts the meeting, and her hand slides over to mine.

She twines our fingers together and squeezes, and the warmth of her palm against mine floods up my arm and through my entire body, melting away all those chilling thoughts I had when I took this seat.

My heart stutters as I look at our entwined hands resting on my thigh.

We've touched each other in so many intimate ways, but somehow, this feels so much more meaningful than anything we've ever done together.

I tip my head toward her, trying to keep my voice low while Manny continues his welcoming thoughts. Her scent fills my lungs, and I breathe her in before I ask the question I probably shouldn't.

"What are you doing here, Ivy?"

She pulls her bottom lip under her teeth and shakes her head, and I see the glisten of unshed tears in her eyes.

Her slender shoulders rise and fall apologetically. "I don't know."

That waver in her voice...

Her unsteady but *honest* admission...

They're enough to tell me all I need to know without her saying another word.

This is all she can give me right now.

Being here with me like this.

Sitting beside me and supporting my recovery by *being* here.

Trying to understand me better, even when she's seen the bad.

And she may not see it the way I do, but it feels like a giant step I didn't realize I've been holding my breath for.

She saw me that night.

In a very dark place.

The worst I had been since I got out of rehab.

So fucking close to breaking.

And she sat there while I unloaded the horrific truth of all that I had done, those things I was never able to admit, even when we were drawn closer by our shared grief.

Ivy saw it that night, how easily I could fall back into being that person who resorts to injecting poison into their veins when the pain becomes too much.

Yet, she's *here.*

She's beside me.

And that's *enough.*

That light at the end of the tunnel that I talked about when I stood in this room the morning after my epic crash seems somehow closer.

More real.

Reachable.

We refocus our attention on the front of the room as Manny finishes his opening remarks, and Riley gets up to speak first. I try to concentrate on his words, on everything he's saying, because it's so fucking important for me to give him the attention and support he does me, but all I can feel is how tightly she's gripping my hand, how warm her body is where her shoulder presses against mine, the slight shifts she makes as she tries to find a more comfortable position on the shitty folding chairs, the sound of every little breath she takes.

She's here…

And by the time Riley finishes and steps down, I feel like I'm about to jump out of my skin.

Because my body craves her.

It wants her just as bad as it did that heroin sitting on the floor beside me that night.

My knee bounces, and when Manny asks who wants to speak next, I raise my hand and push to my feet before anyone else takes that opportunity.

Because I needed to break that connection.

Because she needs to hear the things I talk about here, the things that *will* make her uncomfortable, the things that will show her that this addiction will always be that voice in my head and devil on my shoulder that I'm fighting against.

She was the only thing that kept me from relapsing that night, and she needs to understand how easily I could find myself in that situation again, especially with the twisted emotions that will always follow me where she's concerned.

Ivy's gaze flicks up to me.

I offer her a tight smile and squeeze her hand once before releasing it so I can slip past her and walk up the aisle to the front of the room.

Manny claps me on the shoulder as I turn to face all the familiar people I spend so much time with, who have helped me through everything that's happened since I moved back to Philly, who have never once judged me, despite the fact that I have given them countless reasons to that have nothing to do with my drug use and everything to do with what I've done to Drew and Ivy.

And having her here now somehow makes all those confessions I've made seem obsolete, like they're not nearly enough.

I reach under my shirt and grab my medallion, pulling it free and running my fingers across it. "I know most of you have heard me talk a lot about this, about why I got clean."

My gaze lifts to her, and the way her bottom lip trembles makes me clench the metal even tighter.

"It took a long time for me to realize that getting sober for somebody else was never going to work." I watch her back stiffen, the tears pooling in her eyes. "And not only was I doing it for someone else, but I was doing it for a terrible reason. So that I could hurt the person *I* loved the most in the world, in order to get the person *he* loved the most."

Fuck.

It doesn't matter how many times I've stood up here

and talked about this. Each time I do, the pressure in my chest builds until I can barely breathe and my heart feels like it's being torn apart with each word.

But I make myself do it.

Because every time I discuss what happened, what I did, *why* I made those choices and the ones that led me into full-blown addiction, it reminds me why I can't *ever* go back there.

I can't try to hold in what I'm feeling because it inevitably eats me alive, and I can't drown it with booze or drugs or anything else.

All I can do is face it—no matter how painful it might be.

Like this confession...

"After my brother died, I did my best to keep my distance from the thing that had become my obsession, my *addiction*, from the person who had replaced the drugs." I offer her a sad smile, remembering that first month after Drew's death, when I tried to stay away from her but found myself parked outside her house, wondering if she was okay and fighting the part of me that wanted to go to her. "But I couldn't. I was too weak. And as time went on, my addiction to her and the feeling I got when I was around her only grew, and I continued to make terrible choices where she was concerned."

Like not walking away that night in the alley after she followed me to the meeting...

Not forcing her to heed my warning...

When I kept returning to her house to dig through those boxes looking for that doll, when I could have just asked Mom to do it...

And when I pulled her into my lap that night to comfort her, to comfort *me*, after we said goodbye on that beach, knowing full damn well it was a horrible idea...

"I would love to blame all the terrible things I did on my drug use, but everything that happened with my brother and Ivy I did while I was sober. Except for the night that she saved my life."

A tear trickles down her cheek, but she continues to hold my gaze. Not looking away even when I'm saying the hard things she probably doesn't want to hear.

She *doesn't* look away.

"I broke her with the truth that night, and she saw the addict for the first time. She saw me drunk and on the verge of ending over a year of being clean, all because I couldn't deal with the guilt and pain in any healthy way." I grip the medallion tightly, remembering how I took it off and chucked it across the studio after receiving the package from Drew. "And now, I find myself in an even more difficult position, knowing I should walk away, knowing that it probably isn't healthy." I shake my head, glancing at Dale, who gives me a knowing look after the many conversations we've had about the Ivy situation. "Okay—it *definitely* isn't."

I run my hand through my hair, struggling to find what I want to say.

"But I can't just walk away because even though there are some things I can never make amends for, I've dedicated my life to at least trying where she's concerned. And that means keeping my major trigger—the person I became so obsessed with that I let it control me—*in* my life. It means keeping all the guilt and pain that could make me pick up front and center on a daily basis." I release a mirthless laugh. "And I know what a lot of you would say about that. Especially Dale." I cut my gaze over to him, and he smirks. "But the truth is, it isn't just about Ivy or my feelings for her anymore. My niece will be born before too long…"

My voice breaks, and I swallow at the lump in my throat.

In only a few short months, that miracle baby they tried so hard for, that they never thought would ever happen, will be here in this world. Knowing that makes it easy to bear the burden of the guilt that may never go away. It helps ease the pain even as I know looking at her will bring another wave of it crashing over me.

"Drew won't be here to meet his daughter. And I know I don't have any right to want it, but I need to be there, to help her learn about her father, to tell her all those stories only *I* know so she doesn't miss out on what I took from her."

I draw in a shaky breath and tighten my grip on the medallion to help ground myself to *something*.

"There are some things that can't be forgiven, that can't be fixed, and we all know that. We're told that all we can do is accept responsibility for our actions and that we might never earn forgiveness from everyone we've hurt. But I'm going to keep trying. Even if I fail."

I lift my gaze to find Ivy's in the back row— unwavering.

"And even if one day Ivy comes to her senses and tells me to get fucking lost, I will still keep striving to find a way to make her life better, to make their baby's life whole. Because that's all that we can ever do, right? Try?"

27

CAM

Ivy opens the front door just as I step up onto the porch, as if she's been waiting for me the same way I have been for this moment. For what feels like forever...

Because the first time I stood here, I came to her with guilt I couldn't unload and longing I never thought would amount to anything.

I came to her seeking redemption I didn't think was possible.

And when that package from Drew arrived, I *knew* it wasn't.

But as snow starts to fall and she steps back with bare feet to let me into the home she once shared with him, I can feel the shift in the air that has nothing to do with the flakes hitting my skin.

I don't know what she's thinking after the meeting, after hearing me say all those words. She seemed confused enough about even being there, but now that I've confessed all those things out loud to *her*, it feels like we've reached some sort of breaking point.

Or at the very least, a tipping one.

She retreats as I move in and push the door closed behind me, arms wrapped around herself in an ivory over-sized sweater that falls off one shoulder in a way that makes me very glad she kept her coat on at the meeting.

Her soulful eyes watch me carefully, and she bites her bottom lip, shifting nervously as she rubs at her belly and moves back another step, like she wants or needs to put some physical distance between us.

And that's probably a good idea, given what has happened far more times than it should have between us within these walls.

Even now, that crackling energy that always seems to surge when we're alone together permeates the air between us. Electrifying my skin, making my fingers itch to touch her.

She didn't tell me to come over, didn't say a word after I spoke. She just held my hand for the rest of the meeting and slipped out when it was done, but I couldn't go home like I probably should have.

I couldn't walk away after she showed up like that, when it feels like there are so many things that still need to be said that we've been dancing around for months.

"Why did you come tonight, Ivy?"

The answer she offered me at the meeting was enough for that moment, but now, *here*, I need more.

So much more.

I can't keep pretending that it doesn't break my fucking heart and shatter my soul every time I come over here and touch her and then have to pretend it didn't happen and walk away. I can't keep living day in and day out acting like this can go on indefinitely when we both know it can't.

And the way she's looking at me tells me she knows that as well.

She releases her lip and shakes her head. "I honestly don't know, Cam. It just..." Her eyes drift closed, and she draws in a long breath and releases it slowly, almost like her answer is something she needs to prepare herself for. When her lids flutter open again, there's a steely resolve in her gaze. "It just felt like where I needed to be."

Such simple words that hold so much meaning.

The only time this woman has *willingly* been in a room with me since she learned the truth has been when she needed something *physical* from me. When she was seeking something familiar and comforting that only I could give her. And even then, she let me know that nothing about her feelings had changed, no matter what her body might have wanted.

"Why, Ivy? You've told me over and over again how much you hate me. How much I hurt you. And even when you didn't say those words, I still know they're true. So, why would you want to be there for that? For me?"

That flicker of light I saw, that hint of hope I felt when she entwined her hand with mine, hovers in the distance now, waiting to be fully lit or snuffed out completely.

Tears well in her eyes, and her bottom lip trembles.

"That's what I've been asking myself. I've been trying to find an answer. And then, after last week—"

"Last week?"

She glances down the hallway and gives me a soft smile. "The nursery. I was...confused."

"Why?"

Ivy has to know I'd do *anything* for her by now, that every breath I take is to ensure she and her baby are taken care of the way they deserve to be. So, why would me wanting to do something like that for her be so confusing?

"Because I don't understand how someone who could do something like *that* for me could also have done so many horrible things to Drew."

Her words cut through me like a knife, flaying me open and leaving me bleeding out on her floor.

I try to take a step toward her, to clutch her to me to try to stem the flow and keep myself together, but I stop myself because I'm terrified of doing or saying the wrong thing.

Ivy motions toward Gladys sitting on the end table next to the photo of her with Drew on the beach. "It's hard for me to reconcile those two people, Cam. Who I *know* you are, who you've *shown* me you are, over and over again, and *that* person."

It's a dichotomy that has torn me apart for far longer than Ivy has been in my life. My ability to shut other things and people out to hyper-fixate on a canvas or idea in my head, juxtaposed against my soul-deep love for those people who do mean something in my life and my desire to ensure they have everything they ever need.

She became that focus. To the detriment of everything

and everyone around me. To the detriment of myself. It pulled me away from that other part that was so damn happy for Drew when he met her...before I saw her and everything changed.

It's the part of me that will always struggle with those voices in my head.

"I don't know if I can explain it, Ivy, because that's something I don't understand myself. Every fucking minute of every day, I look back and wonder who the *fuck* that person was who made so many *horrible* decisions and hurt so many people." I shake my head, as if the motion might somehow alleviate some of the pain centered there with the memories. "I know you can't forgive me, Ivy, and it's okay if you never can, but that isn't going to stop *this*."

I motion between us.

A tear slips from her eye, slowly making its way down her cheek. "Stop *what*?"

"Whatever this is between us." My hands tremble as I shove them through my hair. "I can't do it anymore. I can't keep pretending I don't love you with every fucking fiber of my being. That I don't want to be here with you every moment of every fucking day. That it doesn't destroy me every time I walk away from you. That I'm terrified I'm going to miss something important with you, with this baby. That I'm going to miss out on your life, on hers. And believe me, I know how fucking selfish it is to want that when Drew can't have it, but it doesn't mean I don't."

Ivy sobs, crumpling in on herself, and I can't take it anymore.

I close the distance between us and pull her against me, burying my face in her hair as her hands press into my stomach and her forehead falls to my chest, her belly into mine.

Each labored breath, every anguished sound that falls from her lips, makes it harder and harder for me to fight my own tears.

"I don't hate you." She pulls her head back and looks up at me, tears now streaking down her cheeks. "I wanted to so badly." Fingers cling to my shirt, twisting the soft fabric. "I *wanted* to hate you, but even the night you told me everything, I couldn't. If I had, I would have left you to your own devices. I would have let you drink yourself to death or shoot that poison into your veins. I would have gotten my revenge that way, but I *couldn't* hate you."

"Why not?"

I'm terrified of her answer, of what might come out, but I need to know.

"Because it isn't your fault."

Her declaration stiffens my spine.

She can't be saying what I think she is...

"What?"

"I've been blaming you for everything, but it isn't really your fault."

I tighten my hold on her. "Of *course* it is, Ivy—"

"No, Cam." She clutches my shirt tighter, jerking me toward her, forcing me to hold her gaze. "Marlo said something to me last week that stuck, and I haven't been able to stop thinking about it. About everything that happened in minute detail."

The same thing I've been doing for months...

Reliving every word said.

Every action.

Every *thought* that led to this.

Ivy offers me the saddest smile. "It was all just some weird twist of fate." Her eyebrows rise. "Why did I meet Drew first and not you? Why did I go out into the yard alone that night? Why did you find me before Drew did? Why didn't I notice all the things that should have told me you weren't him?" She reaches up and trails her fingers across my cheek. "Why didn't he tell me the truth when he had so much time to? Why was he so afraid? What did I do to make him question that? Why didn't that doll get delivered when my invitation did? Why did I choose to fucking send it? Why did that car have to be crossing that intersection at the exact moment Drew was distracted enough to run the stop sign?"

A sob slips from her lips as all the questions she just asked, ones I've anguished over, continue to float through my head. Each one a single millisecond in time. A chance for things to go differently.

But they didn't.

For some inexplicable reason, *this* is where we ended.

Tears blur my vision, and I blink them away, needing to see her clearly.

"None of it makes sense, Cam, because none of it was in anyone's control. Not really. There are so many variables, and any one of them being different would have changed everything." She huffs out a labored breath. "I can't keep blaming you for all of it. I can't. Because there were so many opportunities for things to turn out differently, which means there's a *reason* they turned out like *this*."

One of her hands slips down between us to press against her swollen belly.

"Maybe this baby wouldn't have happened if everything else hadn't." The corner of her lips tips up. "Maybe she is my chance to let go of all of this pain and anger because holding it in feels like constantly drinking poison." Her eyes search mine. "I can't keep acting like I don't love you."

All the air rushes from my lungs as I stare down at her.

She loves me.

I've longed to hear those words for so many fucking years, struggled through so many nights I didn't think I'd survive, wanting them, but now that she's said them, I have a hard time believing it.

A hard time understanding.

"You love me..."

She offers me a sad smile and pushes up to feather her lips across mine gently. "God fucking help me, but I do. Remember how you told me that kissing me tasted like red, that I brought color back into your life?"

I nod.

"Well, kissing you brought me back to life. If you hadn't shown up on my doorstep that night, I don't know where I'd be. I don't know that I'd be here. Or that Drew's daughter would be about to come into this world."

I gaze at her through the haze of tears and capture her face between my palms, sweeping my thumb across her trembling lips.

Ones I've kissed.

Ones I've craved.

Ones I've fought so hard to forget.

But now they've brought me the most beautiful words I've ever heard from the only woman in the world who has ever held my heart.

"I'm going to make sure she knows who her dad was and how much he loves her. And I promise you, Ivy, I'm going to love the two of you enough for the both of us."

28

CAM

Ivy stares up at me with so much affection in her soft gaze that it feels like I might drown under the weight of it.

I'm not sure I'm ever going to believe I deserve it.

No matter how long this lasts, no matter how long she puts up with me and all the bullshit I carry with me, the fact that a woman like Ivy, who has suffered so much because of my actions, can still look at me like *this* feels like a dream I'll be ripped away from at any moment.

I've lived with nightmares for so many years. The kind that had me wake screaming, drenched in sweat, my body craving all those horrible things I gave it. They became what I expected, and after Drew died and I learned the truth of what I had done, they only got worse.

Darker.

More demanding.

But this offer in her gaze is all warmth and light.

She pushes up onto her toes and skimming her lips

across mine, running her fingers through my hair. "I know you will."

Just feeling her hands on me again is enough to make my cock harden where it's pinned between her belly and mine.

I've missed *this* touch.

The one filled with affection and compassion instead of anger and hate.

It makes heat ripple across every inch of my skin and warms me in a way nothing else can.

When she pulls back, a tear trickles down her cheek.

I dip my head and kiss it away, the saltiness splashing against my lips, and all I want is to be here to kiss away every single tear she ever sheds. "I love you, Ivy, and I can't promise things will ever be perfect, that *I* ever will be, because I'm far from it. But I promise I will do anything and everything for you and this baby until the day that I die. Anything you ask, anything you need."

"What about what *you* need?"

Her question makes my heart skip a beat, because it's been so long since I've asked myself that or even considered it.

But it's an easy one to answer.

I take her face between my palms, cradling her soft cheeks. "You and this baby are all that I need. To know that you're safe and happy, and you might not be right now, but we'll get there. I know we can."

That is my hope.

That one day, all this pain won't cripple us. Open wounds will close. Scabs will heal. Scars will form. And they will still ache, probably forever. But they won't destroy us the way they do now.

I won't let them.

She nods, leaning into my touch. "We can."

And then her mouth is on mine again.

I kiss her fiercely, in the way I've so badly wanted to over the last several months but haven't been able to because I couldn't *tell* her I loved her. I couldn't *show* her I did. That wasn't what she needed or wanted in any of those moments.

She wanted the *feeling*—the physical one, not all the emotional baggage we both carry with us, not reminders of all the reasons what we were doing should never have happened.

But now all of that has changed because we've changed.

Because we've finally been able to move past that point where the agony and guilt were at their highest point, when it felt like there was no way around them and no way to ever come back from it.

Yet somehow, we made it over that sharp peak.

We passed that breaking point, cutting ourselves deeply on the shards of the lives we had before, but we came out *alive.*

We're on our way back down the other side.

Hopefully a little wiser and a little more ready to deal with all the things we're going to have to face. The hard questions that we'll both have to continue to ask ourselves, maybe for the rest of our lives, about why things turned out like this.

But we'll do it *together.*

Because we're stronger like this—tethered together by the twisted, intersecting strands of fate woven by some unknown hands rather than getting trapped by their binds as we fight against them.

Ivy gives herself over completely to the kiss, a little mewl coming from the back of her throat. I groan in response, knowing full well what that sound means, what she wants, and it's exactly what I need, too.

Only, I want it to be different from the way it has been between us this entire time.

Even those first few nights we had together before the shit hit the fan, I was still holding back, continuing to hide things from her—about my past, about myself, about what I had done—but now that she knows everything, I can truly let her see all of me and what I really feel about her and this baby.

How much I love them and need them in my life.

She pulls away abruptly and takes my hand in hers, tugging on it to lead me down the hallway toward the bedroom that I've walked out of so many nights feeling like absolute shit because of what I had done for her, because of what it was doing to *me*.

It broke me down the more I came to make *her* feel good.

But now, she actually wants me there in that bed with her.

She wants to be in my arms. It's no longer just a way to forget, but a way to make promises about the future, a way to cement how we feel about each other and where all this is going, what it all means.

It may be too early to really know that or even

attempt to unravel the depth of those feelings that live inside us, but we can sort through them together as long as we *try*.

And I will *never* stop trying.

Ivy stops at the edge of the bed and releases my hand, reaching for the hem of her sweater, but I catch her wrist, shaking my head.

"No." I brush my lips across her cheek to her ear. "Let me do it. I want to see all of you like this."

With the lights on.

Without the dark cloud hanging over me thinking she hated me.

All I want to do is drink her in.

Because Christ, she's beautiful pregnant, even more so than she was before, which I didn't think was even possible.

The way her entire body seems to glow, her breasts higher and fuller, the swell of her belly and knowing she's growing a life in there. I run my hand across it, pressing my palm over the center, and the baby kicks, a tiny foot pressing into my touch.

I grin at her and another tear slides down her cheek.

Her lips curl. "I think she likes your voice."

A blazing warmth floods my chest, and somehow, it feels like my heart stops and beats faster at the same time.

I didn't know how badly I needed to hear that, to know that my niece *feels* something for me even before she's entered this world. That I am going to have a chance to watch her grow and thrive and become everything that Drew would want her to be.

Tears prick my eyes, but I blink them away and

manage to swallow through the tightness in my throat. "I hope so because she's going to be hearing a lot of it."

Because I plan to spend every waking moment I can with this woman and this baby.

Being whatever they need.

Giving them the world.

Ensuring they have anything they could ever want.

Ivy laughs at my comment, and it's filled with something I wasn't sure I would ever hear from her again—joy, maybe hope for the future, and faith that in the end, it won't just be agony and anger but love and hope that pulls us through the hard days.

Today started out as one of them.

When I walked into that meeting, I was nearing my breaking point with Ivy.

After weeks of keeping it all in, giving her what she needed while I tried to ignore how badly it was affecting me, and then showing her the nursery, pretending it wasn't pure torture to walk away that night was getting to be impossible.

But I don't have to pretend anymore.

I don't have to hold back.

And I won't.

Not ever again with her.

I grab the hem of her sweater and slowly glide it up over her stomach, her breasts, and pull it free, letting it fall to the floor. Her long, dark hair spills out, and I grasp a strand of it, letting the silky texture skate over my skin.

My hands itch to touch every single inch of her, but I force myself to hold back, to instead allow only my gaze to rake over her. From her warm, welcoming gaze, to her slightly parted lips swollen from our kissing, and down over the swell of her breasts peeking out of her bra.

I trail my fingertips along the edge of the material, and she shivers, inching closer until her belly presses into mine again.

Resting her hands on my chest, she leans in. "You know what I just realized?"

Her voice wavers, but the unsteadiness has nothing to do with fear or trepidation and everything to do with the fact that she's just as on edge as I am.

"What?"

"I've never gotten to really see you naked." I narrow my eyes on her and she smirks, sliding a hand down to tease them along the hem of my T-shirt, making my skin pebble with goosebumps. "You were always so focused on me, so intent that you never gave me a chance to explore *you.*"

I grin at her. "Well, now you have it." Dipping my head, I drag my lips over her temple. "All the time in the fucking world..."

She pulls at the material, and I take a step back, reaching behind me to tug it off in one smooth motion. I toss it onto the floor and stand in front of her, suddenly feeling exposed in a way I never have before.

Her warm eyes move over me, across my chest to my NA medallion hanging from my neck. She reaches out and grabs it, running her fingers across it. "How come I've never seen this before?"

My old, familiar friend guilt tries to push its way into my head, but I fight to force it back. "I take it off while I paint so it doesn't get anything on it."

"What about when you're not painting?"

She's referring to the many times we've been together here, when she's asked me to come over, when she's needed me...

"I took it off when I came over here because it always felt like I was picking back up, like I was doing something wrong and giving into something that I knew was hurting me."

Her gaze softens, an apology soaked in the wetness brimming around them. "I'm sorry I made you feel that way..."

"Don't." I press my thumb across her lips, silencing her. "Don't apologize for something I freely gave you. I *wanted* to be here, Ivy. I knew what I was doing. Don't feel guilty about anything that's happened between us."

It takes a few moments before she nods and returns her focus to examining me, her gaze drifting down my torso, and she dips her head to the side and grabs my hand, lifting it to examine the twining black and white snakes that swirl up my left arm. "What do these mean?"

My body starts to tremble as she examines them more closely, taking in every minute detail of the artwork I've worn on my skin for over a decade.

I swallow thickly, and her eyes flick up to meet mine in question. "They're how I always saw Drew and me. I got this shortly after we graduated high school. When he went off to college, so sure of himself and his path to medical school, and I kind of..."—I shrug—"I knew I wanted to do the art thing, but I didn't have much direction."

Her brow furrows. "But you went to art school?"

"Eventually." I nod. "It didn't happen right away, though."

She trails a finger over the dark snake, and then over the light one. "Which one is you?"

I can't help the little laugh that slips from my lips. "Do you really have to ask that?"

Her gaze immediately flicks up to mine. "Of course I do."

The sincerity in her words makes it hard to say what should be so obvious. "I think we both know that Drew was the light in this world, and I was the shadow."

She shakes her head as tears well in her eyes. "That's not true. You brought light back into my world when it was at its darkest."

"Then I snuffed it out again..."

Ivy presses her lips together firmly like she's trying to fight back a sob. "That light was still there. It was just hidden by all the guilt and anger and pain." She reaches up and takes my face in her small, soft palm. "I don't want you to ever see yourself as only one thing, Cam. Just like your paintings, you're not all black and white. There are a thousand different shades of gray in them, and there are in you, too. And in me, and in everyone else."

A tear slips from my eye, and she quickly swipes it away and kisses me softly before she moves her hand down to the small tattoo on my rib cage to examine it.

She pulls back with a raised brow. "That definitely isn't what I was expecting..."

I smirk at her.

The two broken hearts with the word "crybaby"

written across them have sat there for almost as long as the snakes have wound on my arm.

Her gaze flicks up from it. "You definitely need to explain this one to me."

My lips twitch as I try to contain a smile at the flood of memories that come with that ink. "That's what Drew used to call me."

Wide, horrified eyes meet mine. "What?"

I chuckle. "Not in a hurtful way. I mean, it was at the beginning, but we were very young. I was always really emotional as a child, and I used to cry all the time."

"And then things kind of switched when your dad died."

I narrow my gaze on her. "Yeah, but how did you—"

"Your mom told me..."

Of course she did.

The relationship Mom and Ivy share is special, something I'm so happy they both have after Drew's death, but sometimes, there are things that are better left unsaid. And I never know what kind of secrets—embarrassing or otherwise—Mom might spill to her.

Though, this one doesn't sting as much as some of the others because I *want* Ivy to know this part of me, to help her understand why I am the way I am and why I turned to alcohol and drugs to cope with all those feelings I couldn't deal with after what I did in Mom's garden.

"I kind of shut down emotionally when we lost him, kept it all in, and Drew became the one who was much more open with his feelings. So, I started throwing the insult back at him, and it kind of became, I don't know, a joke between us."

Her lips curl into a soft smile, and she coasts her fingers across it, making me shudder and my cock ache at the gentle touch. "Are these the only tattoos you have?"

I shake my head, unease creeping across the back of my neck. "No, I have a newer one."

"You do?"

Trepidation tightens my skin until it feels like it might rupture because I don't know how Ivy will take this one.

But there isn't any way to hide it from her, nor do I want to.

No more hiding.

I slowly turn and let her see my other ribcage and the ink I got there after the night she saved my life.

When she became even more to me than I thought possible...

Ivy sucks in a sharp breath. "Is that..."

I nod. "A peony. Whenever I see them, I think of you."

The tears that had pooled in her eyes earlier fall now, and she nods. "They're my favorite."

"I know." I slide my fingers under her chin and tilt her face up toward me. "And I knew that no matter what happened between us, even if you eventually told me to get the fuck out of your life for good, that I would never be able to fully walk away, that I would always want part of you with me. You saved me, Ivy, and now, I'll have you with me forever, no matter what, as a reminder of what you did for me that night."

29

CAM

I can't miss the tiny flicker of doubt that flashes in her eyes with my words, the reminder that this might not be forever the way we want it to be, and I can't say I blame her after everything we've been through.

She could very well tell me tomorrow that this is all a huge mistake. That she got caught up in the moment and floated along on a tide of attraction that can't wash away all the bad feelings and events of our pasts.

But I have to start living in the moment and planning a future where things *do* work out because if I stay grounded in the past, I'm never going to move out of it.

We'll *both* stay trapped in the pain and grief.

I slide my hands around her, hugging her as tightly to me as I can. "I will never walk away from you unless you ask me to, Ivy. I'm not going anywhere."

Another tear slowly trails down her cheek, and I kiss it away, fighting against my own. Because if I don't, the floodgates will open and I won't be able to stop the tsunami of emotions I've been holding in for so long.

Goosebumps break out over her skin as I skim my fingertips along her back to unhook her bra. She leans into my touch, shivering as I drag it down her arms and let it fall to the floor.

I walk her back the final two steps until her legs bump the bed. Capturing her face in my palms, I kiss her deeply as I slowly lower her back onto it. She groans, her tongue sweeping along mine, her body shifting restlessly.

Pulling away, I feather my lips over her cheek. "Is it too uncomfortable for you on your back right now?"

She shakes her head. "I'm okay for a little while."

I lift my head and smirk at her. "When have you ever known me to only take a little while?"

Her laughter fills the room, the sound flooding my heart and soul with so much joy that it fully brings me back into the moment. All those hints of uncertainty I saw in her gaze are completely gone now, washed away by my promise.

The longer I stare into her eyes, the more I kiss her lips, the further I slide my hands down to the waistband of her pants, the more my cock throbs to be inside her, to feel her pussy clenching and rippling as she comes.

I tug on the stretchy fabric, dragging it down and off her feet along with her panties, leaving her gloriously naked in front of me.

Sweet fucking hell...

She's so beautiful that it makes my chest ache.

But not with the type of blistering agony I've felt for months.

It's a warmth that spreads out from my heart and engulfs every inch of me.

A feeling only Ivy could ever bring.

I drift my hands across her collarbone, down the V between her breasts, across her smooth, round belly, and slowly dip my fingers between her thighs.

She arches into the touch, her cunt already slick with need.

Her hands curl into the sheets, clasping them beneath her as she shifts restlessly.

I push up to my feet and lean over her, pressing my lips to hers. "I am going to devour you, Ivy. And then when I'm done, I'm going to make love to you."

Her breath hitches.

Her eyes meet mine, clouded and full of desire.

And for the first time since we've been together, there's absolutely no reservation there.

There's nothing being held back.

There's no anger.

It doesn't mean it won't return, that there won't be times she hates me because of the past or some other mistake I'll make in the future, but right now, she doesn't.

I have her here fully present, fully with *me*, and I will not lose out on it.

Pushing my fingers into her, I curl them into that soft, fleshy spot that makes her squirm and capture her gasp, swallowing it greedily as I do *everything* that is Ivy.

Because there is no getting enough of her, enough of *this*.

Her pussy contracts, and I growl my approval as I slowly sink to my knees at the edge of the bed and tug her legs over my shoulders, giving me better access to her.

Christ...I could keep my face buried between this woman's legs forever and die a very happy man.

Never needing anything else.

Never wanting anything else but her.

Ivy clutches the comforter tightly, and I glide my tongue across her damp flesh. Her taste coats it and slides down my throat. My rumbled groan of appreciation makes her hips buck, and I slowly repeat the move, exploring her, delving deep inside and alternating it with quick flicks of the tip of my tongue across her clit that have her bowing up off the mattress.

I place my free hand gently across her stomach to keep her down, to hold her in place as I thrust my finger into her in a languid rhythm I mirror with my attention on the apex of her thighs.

Taking my time.

Slowly building her up toward her release.

There's nothing rushed about tonight.

There won't be anything rushed again between us unless we want it to be because things have finally started to settle into place.

It may not be how we imagined the future would look when we met for the first time—or should I say when *she* thought we met for the first time—on that dark and stormy night when her world had fallen so completely apart. But it's the future we have, the one we have to accept and live with or we'll be swallowed whole by the black hole of pain we've been stuck in due to the past.

Her hips start to roll as I suck her clit between my lips

and pulse in time with my finger. She whimpers, her hands clinging to the comforter even tighter. Every muscle of her body trembles and tenses, and then she's coming on a silent cry.

Her breath hitching.

Her body convulsing.

Her pussy grinding against my face, thighs clamping around my head and twisting slightly.

And I drink her all down every last drop, dragging my tongue over her and probing in so I don't waste even a single taste.

When she finally sags down onto the bed, I slide up and lean over her again to see her darkened cheeks that I imagine are a brilliant shade of pink or maybe even red at this point.

A grin pulls in my mouth. "Fucking beautiful…"

The words come out on a low growl, and I press my hard cock, still encased in my jeans, against her slick core.

She groans, her head lolling back and her hips moving against my length.

Her eyes flutter open and she looks up at me, the tiniest grin playing at her lips. "I have to get off my back."

I nod and slowly slide my hands under her to help her sit up.

She braces herself up on the edge of the bed, and I step back and reach for the zipper of my jeans. Her eyes never leave me the entire time as I lower it, then slide the denim down, and pull them off, tossing them with the rest of our clothes.

Her bottom lip disappears under her teeth as her eyes

zero in on my cock in a way that makes pre-cum leak from the head of it.

"If you keep looking at me like that, Ivy, I won't last very long."

Her gaze flicks up to meet mine and she releases her lip, grinning.

I kneel in front of her, gripping her chin in my fingers. "I've told you before how often I fantasized about you taking my cock between these lips." My thumb glides across the bottom one that still bears the imprint of her teeth. "And coming down your throat." I glide my hand down there and hold her. She swallows against it, the motion enough to make my dick jump thinking about feeling that motion along it. "But not right now. Later. After I've made you come at least two more times."

She issues a little whimper at my promise and lets me tug her up from the bed and into my arms. I kiss her as I walk her backward until her shoulders hit the wall behind her near the windows.

"Turn around and put your hands flat against that wall."

Her eyes flare, but she nods and turns, placing her palms as I instructed and looking at me over her left shoulder.

Thick, dark hair spills down her back, and I trail my fingers through it as I drop to my knees behind her and drag my mouth across her lower back and her ass.

I kiss every inch of her I can reach until her body quivers again, and I slide my hand up between her legs, finding her slick both with her release and her continued arousal. "You're ready for me?"

She nods, her hooded gaze burning with the same desire coursing through my veins, and I push up and grasp her hips, tugging them back until she's bent forward enough to give me perfect access to her.

With her ass in the air like this, offering herself to me, it might be the sexiest thing I've ever seen in my life. And I commit it to memory so I can paint this exact moment in time forever.

I slide my right hand around her stomach to help hold her steady and support her and use my left to guide my cock to her slick core. She groans as I drag it through her wetness, coating myself completely, and I push in on one torturously slow thrust.

Bloody hell...

Her tight cunt grips me, and her eyes roll back in her head, her mouth falling open in a silent gasp as I'm seated fully inside her.

"Fuck..." My groan tumbles from my lips against her ear, and she releases a heavy breath as if she's been holding it. "You good?"

She nods, arching back and clamping down on me in a way that makes my balls draw up tight and threaten to unload.

Jesus...

This woman...

I drag my hips back and plunge into her again, setting a pace that will build up slowly just like before, proving to her that we don't have to rush anything anymore. She takes each thrust, clenching around me on every withdrawal, her hips moving in time with mine.

We roll seamlessly together, like the waves crashing along the shore.

Pressing my chest to her back, I kiss her cheek, the corner of her lips, everything I can get my mouth on. "God, you take my cock so beautifully, Ivy."

She mewls and clamps around my length so hard I have to grit my teeth to keep from coming on the spot.

"Fuck, woman."

I draw my hips back and slam into her again a little harder this time.

A gasp falls from her parted lips, and she nods. "Yes, like that."

Increasing the tempo, her body moves back to meet mine, demanding more, seeking the same thing I am—for her to come unraveled.

I slide my left hand down to grasp her thigh and lift her leg up and back, changing the angle slightly and allowing me to get even deeper. And the sound that comes from her is unlike anything I've ever heard before.

Raw.

Feral.

And I can't hold back anymore.

I plunge into her relentlessly, carefully keeping one hand supporting her, as hers seek purchase against the wall.

"Anything you want." *Thrust.* "Anytime." *Thrust.* "Anywhere, Ivy." *Thrust.* "Forever." *Thrust.* "You know that, don't you?"

She nods, unable to respond verbally as I continue to drive into her.

The sound of her frantic whimpers, our bodies

coming together, and my own panting breaths fill the room, and I can't take it anymore.

I slide my right hand from her belly down to find her clit and twist it in my fingers.

Ivy comes on a sharp cry that echoes in my ears as her clasping cunt finally draws out my release.

The one I've been holding back for months that contains all my love, all my pain, all my guilt and regret.

It leaves me on a roar as I come deep inside her with uneven thrusts.

I clutch her tightly, keeping her upright even though my own legs tremble beneath me, and when we both come down, I allow her foot to slide back down to the floor and tug her back all the way, pressing her into my chest.

Her head lolls back against my shoulder, and I ghost a kiss across her temple.

We stand like this for what feels like forever.

Both of us pant, trying to catch our breaths.

Her heart thunders under my palm centered over it as mine does against her back.

I nuzzle her ear. "I'm going to take you into the shower now, and you're going to come again. And then I'm going to fall asleep with you wrapped in my arms, and I'm not leaving tonight."

Half-lidded, lust-soaked eyes meet mine. "No, you aren't."

30

CAM

Ivy stumbles into the kitchen with her dark hair disheveled from sleep—and other things—and yawns, pressing the back of her hand over her mouth.

I glance at the clock on the stove in front of me. Almost nine o'clock. "You okay?"

Her brow furrows. "Yeah?" She rubs at her lower back. "Why wouldn't I be?"

The ease with which she responds and that fact that I don't hear even a *hint* of reservation in her voice helps relieve some of the tension that's been coiled inside every muscle in my body since I woke this morning in *their* bed with Ivy in my arms.

It should have been a moment to relish, to cherish, to luxuriate in as she lay there with her hair spread out across the pillow looking like a damn fucking angel. But the very real fear that she would wake and regret everything we said and did last night wouldn't let me.

And I've been waiting all morning to see her face, to be able to look into her eyes and know she still *wants* this.

She does.

That's enough to make my lips pull into a grin as I motion with the spatula to the clock above the sink. "Because I have never known you to sleep until nine a.m."

Her eyes widen slightly. "Shit, it's that late?"

"Yeah." I nod, fighting a full-blown smile at the adorable, bewildered look on her face. "You clearly needed the sleep."

The tiniest grin curls her lips, and her cheeks darken. And I find myself wondering again about what color they actually are when they're like this—soft peach, bright pink, a striking red... "Yeah, well, someone kept me up last night."

I snort as I turn back to flip the bacon sizzling in the griddle pan. "You're welcome."

"I wasn't complaining."

My cheeks heat and my cock stirs at the sensual tone in her voice and as the memories of making love to her and everything that came after it replay in my head.

It was so different from all the other times we've been together.

So *real.*

Neither of us holding anything back.

No secrets.

No lies.

None of those barriers that existed between us before.

It was *perfect.*

Ivy shuffles around the counter over to me and rests her face against my bare back, wrapping her arms around me tightly. Her belly presses into me, and the baby kicks, making me jump slightly.

She chuckles. "You felt that?"

"How could I miss it?"

Her smile warms my skin. "I told you...she likes your voice. Whenever you're here, she's always more active..."

Hearing that again does that same strange thing to my chest. Makes my heart skip a beat and speed up at the same time.

Something that should be impossible.

About as impossible as the moment we're having right now.

One that seems so easy.

So natural.

Something I thought we would never be able to find.

She kisses my shoulder blade. "That bacon smells amazing."

I manage to shake off the emotion that momentarily froze me in place and blink away the tears burning in my eyes. "It's almost done, and I have pancake batter ready to throw on next."

"No baby-sized fruit?"

Chuckling, I set down the spatula and turn around in her hold so I can take her face in my palms and tuck her unruly hair behind her ears. "About that. It turns out the twenty-seven twenty-eight week range is basically heads of cauliflower, cabbage, or lettuce, and I figured none of those really sounded like a fabulous breakfast option."

She grins at me. "You would be right. Pancakes and bacon sound much better. I've been craving bacon like crazy lately."

"I know." I smirk. "I saw that you bought three packs of it."

A tiny giggle slips from her lips, the sound lifting me higher than any drug ever could.

I lower my forehead to hers and just hold her for a moment, with the sound of the bacon popping and crackling behind us and our hearts beating against each other. "I love you so much."

Her arms tighten around me. "I know. I love you, too."

Pulling my head back, I drift my thumb over her bottom lip. "This isn't going to be easy."

Far from it.

Because even though I didn't want to see it or admit it, Dale was right about so many of the things that trigger me being tied to Ivy.

It will always be a battle against those voices, that faceless enemy, but somehow, with her here at my side, it doesn't feel so unwinnable. I won't be staring down that enemy alone.

She nods. "I know, but nothing that's good ever is, right?"

"It was easy for you and Drew."

Maybe I shouldn't have said it.

The instant that darkness crosses her gaze, I wish I hadn't.

But she gives me a sad smile. "That wasn't always true. I didn't get to see him very much. He was always at work. But I knew he was doing it for a very good reason, that it was his passion to help others. It was part of what I loved so much about him. You and I just have...different complications."

I shake my head. "I don't want to bring more complication into your life, Ivy."

All I want is to make it easier, happier, fulfilling.

"You haven't, Cam." She offers a slight shrug. "I'm not looking at it like that anymore, neither of us can."

I draw in a deep breath and nod, then dip my head to kiss her.

It's slow and sweet.

A savoring of something so beautiful and pure that I definitely don't deserve it.

She leans into my hold, her mouth moving over mine, and a tiny groan slips from her lips.

Good God...

I fucking love that sound.

Even more so when I'm buried inside her or she's coming on my tongue.

But the popping sound behind me reminds me that I was in the middle of doing something before this stunning woman distracted me so thoroughly.

Reluctantly, I pull my head back. "I need to get this bacon off."

She slips away from me and leans against the counter, watching and slowly rubbing at the spot on her belly where the baby seems to kick the most.

I glance back as I take off the crispy pieces and place them on a plate. "She *is* really active this morning, huh?"

She grins and looks down. "Yeah, she is."

"Does it hurt?"

Her laugh floats through the kitchen, and she shakes her head, sending those dark, untamed locks flying. "Not really. At least, not yet. I'm sure when she gets bigger and there's less space in here, it's going to be a lot more uncomfortable. Occasionally, she'll kick my bladder, or something else that certainly doesn't feel great, but I wouldn't say it hurts. It's more like a reminder of, 'Hey, Mom, I'm here.' Like I could ever forget that when—"

The doorbell ringing jerks both of our heads that direction.

I raise a brow. "We're you expecting someone this morning?"

Ivy's eyes widen, panic lacing them. "Oh, shit!"

"What?"

She slaps a hand over her mouth. "Shit, shit, shit!"

"Ivy..."

Her hand falls away, and she gapes. "It's your *mom*."

Fuck.

"Really?"

She nods, her anxious gaze darting between me and the door, then back. "I totally forgot we were supposed to go shopping today, and like you said, I don't usually sleep in this late. I assumed I'd be ready to go by nine."

I run a hand through my hair. "Well, this could get awkward..."

Her bottom lip disappears under her teeth, and she shifts nervously. "What do we do?"

Something I should have done right from the beginning of all this—tell the fucking truth and face the fallout.

I walk over to Ivy and drop kiss on her forehead. "It'll be fine."

She doesn't look wholly convinced, but I can't make Mom stand out there on the porch in this cold weather any longer just so we can try to come up with some way to explain why I'm here.

It wouldn't matter if we did; Nancy Usher would see right through it.

I've kept her in the dark about what has been going on with Ivy the last few months because she wouldn't have understood it and would have been Team Dale—insistent that I cut off at least the sexual part of our relationship. But everything changed literally overnight. And there's no use hiding from the truth anymore.

I make my way to the door and tug it open.

Mom jerks back slightly, her eyes wide as they take in my jeans, bare chest, and unruly hair that clearly suggest I spent the night here. "Oh, Cam...I..."—she tilts her head slightly, her brow furrowing—"wasn't expecting to see you."

"I bet not."

She steps inside the house, and I pull her in for a hug and kiss her cheek.

"Cam, what's going on?"

She tries to whisper it, but I know Ivy is standing in the kitchen behind us, just out of her vision but not out of earshot.

"We'll talk later."

I'm not about to delve into my complicated relationship status with Ivy when I'm not entirely sure what it is either.

But it's *something*.

There's no more pretending it isn't.

And that's a very good start.

I pull out of her hold, and Mom walks past me as I close the door.

Ivy appears from the kitchen with a plastered-on smile that shows all her unease. "Hey, Nancy. I'm so sorry. I overslept, so I'm not ready."

Mom's shrewd gaze sweeps over her in her tiny sleep shorts and one of Drew's old T-shirts she slept in, the disheveled hair, then to me, and she smirks. "It's all right. I'm not in any rush today."

Thank God...

If Mom had decided to press either of us, I'm not sure how well it would have gone when this is still so new.

Yet, somehow, it also *isn't*.

Being here with Ivy like this feels so *right*.

When I first came back to Philly, I sat outside this house, watched her and envied the home Drew and Ivy shared. It's why setting foot inside was so hard after he was gone. But Ivy wants me here, even if there might always be a part of me that feels guilty about it.

"What do you two ladies have planned?"

Mom's face lights up, her lips pulling into a grin. "We're going to look for a stroller and a car seat, and a few other things for the baby's room."

Ivy nods, looking just as excited. "I've been checking out stuff online, but it's so hard to tell without seeing it in person, you know?"

I nod slowly. "Sort of. I wouldn't have been able to select the furniture for the nursery if Mom hadn't helped. Too many options and things I don't understand about what a baby needs."

Which is why I've spent months reading various

books, trying to prepare myself in case Ivy ever let me back into her life again.

Mom chuckles and sets her purse on the end table next to Gladys. "I'm always happy to help. And I don't mind waiting until you're ready, Ivy."

I motion back into the kitchen. "I was just making breakfast. Pancakes and bacon. You want some?"

Waving me off, she shakes her head. "I already ate, but I wouldn't turn down a cup of coffee."

"I can do that."

She settles on the couch, and I slip past Ivy, dragging my hand gently across her stomach and squeezing her hip before I head to the coffee maker.

"You're coming with us, right?"

Ivy's question floats over to me, soft, unsure, but powerful enough to make my knees wobble.

My hand freezes with the pod halfway to the coffee maker, and I squeeze my eyes closed, swallowing through a tight throat. "You want me to come shopping for the baby?"

I'm too afraid to look at her and see what's on her face or in her eyes right now. Terrified I'll break down completely if I so much as glance her direction.

Soft footsteps move across the kitchen, and she sidles up next to me at the counter. Her warm hand slides across my bare back, and she presses up on her toes so she can get close to my ear. "Of course I do."

That light at the end of the tunnel gets brighter.

That hope flickers more solidly.

The churning dark waters it feels like I've been hopelessly treading in for so fucking long start to calm.

I swallow all the things I want to say to Ivy but can't while Mom is seated in the other room. "I'd love to."

Ivy presses a kiss to cheek. "Good. I'm going to go sit with your mom. Let me know if you need any help."

"I'm good." I pour out some batter. "I may not be a master chef, but I can handle pancakes and bacon."

An amused grin plays at her lips that suggests she has some reservations about me in the kitchen—which would be completely fair. "I'm sure you can."

She slips away, leaving me standing stunned.

The ease with which she just invited me to do something so important with her somehow makes all the months of angst and turmoil worth it. Because she wants me around. Not just for herself, but to be in this baby's life, and that's all I've ever wanted since the moment she told me about her.

To be there for *both* of them.

To make up for everything I caused them to lose.

Starting with breakfast...

I start the Keurig and move to the stove to flip the pancakes. Mom and Ivy chat in the living room, occasional laughter hitting my ears and making me grin as I work on our breakfast. It doesn't take long for them to finish cooking, and by the time they're ready, so is the coffee.

"Mom, your coffee's ready."

"Oh, great!" She pushes up from the couch, interrupting whatever conversation she and Ivy were having, and moves into the kitchen, stopping next to me where I plate up breakfast for us. A knowing grin tugs at her lips. "So, you two seem..."

I clear my throat, glancing at Ivy, who seems intent on looking at something on Mom's phone. "I don't know, Mom, but yeah, it does seem that way."

It's all I can say right now.

Just like I don't want to get *my* hopes up, I don't want to do that to Mom, either. After everything she lost, all the pain she's suffered, she deserves something good as much as Ivy does, but I can't promise her something that could be gone tomorrow so easily.

I could fuck it up again.

I could relapse.

And it could rightfully scare Ivy away.

"Hey, Cam?" Ivy pushes up from the couch awkwardly and walks over to us, flipping the phone around so I can see the screen. "Could you paint something like this?"

The nursery in the advertisement has the baby's name written in stars across the night sky on the wall of a nursery.

It would be incredible in the room.

"Of course. As soon as you decide on a name, I can add it to the mural or put it on one of the other walls. Whatever you want."

Ivy smiles and rubs her free hand on her stomach. "I have a name."

Mom's eyes widen. "You do?"

"I've kind of been waiting to tell you guys, but it's going to be Andrea. Drea, for short."

The vise around my chest tightens, and my eyes immediately fill with burning tears.

Fuck.

Mom releases a little sobbing noise as she pulls Ivy

into her arms and hugs her tightly. "Oh, that's beautiful. That's perfect."

Ivy's eyes meet mine over Mom's shoulder, and I don't bother trying to fight the tear that slips down my cheek.

She's naming her after Drew...

Nothing else would have felt right the way this does.

When Mom finally releases her, I step in and tug Ivy up against me. At this point, I don't care if Mom sees us and the questions start coming.

I can't *not* touch her, hold her, after she revealed that.

Ivy stares up at me with an uncertain smile and searching eyes. "What do you think of the name?"

"I think it's absolutely perfect."

Just like the baby will be.

The perfect mix of Ivy and Drew.

I take her face between my hands and angle it up so I can ghost my lips across hers. "She will never want for anything. That promise I made you applies to your daughter, too."

She clings to me, her warm hands pressed directly over my thundering heart. Her eyes fill with tears, and she opens and closes her mouth a few times, searching for whatever she wants to say. "I'm so sorry about everything..."

"No." I shake my head. "Never apologize to me for anything you did or said. The apologies are all mine to give. Forever, if that's what it takes."

This woman has always been my obsession, my addiction, the one thing capable of making me do equally terrible or beautiful things, and now that we've finally reached this place, I will do whatever it takes to keep us like this.

"Forever..." The word comes out barely a whisper, then she smiles. "I thought my agony after losing Drew would last that long, but you've proven to me that the only way to move forward is one second, one minute, one hour, one day at a time. That isn't so scary anymore"—one of her hands slides up my arm and she twines her fingers with mine against her cheek—"because I have you by my side. And together, we can withstand any storm."

EPILOGUE
CAM

NINE MONTHS LATER

Stepping into the Philadelphia Art Museum usually calms me.

The familiar smell of all the old paintings, the worn floors from the constant foot traffic, the hushed conversations and the tour guides walking past, describing all the masterpieces to everyone gawking at them and snapping photos.

It's comfortable.

But today, I'm tense, anxiety coiling around my spine and stiffening it the moment we enter.

Ivy rifles through the bag hanging on the back of the stroller, falling behind me slightly.

I stop walking and turn toward her. "What are you looking for?"

She glances up, frustration in the little huff that puffs from her lips. "Her pacifier in case she wakes up."

Her nervous rustling around, searching for it makes me grin, and I peek down at Drea sleeping soundly in my arms, snuggled against my chest. "I don't think we have to worry about that. She's out cold."

Ivy sighs. "Of course she is, because you're holding her. You know she'll have to get used to sleeping in the stroller or her own crib—*not* in your arms—eventually."

"Well, that day isn't today."

I adjust my hold on Drea to keep her head up, and Ivy rolls her eyes slightly at the same argument we've been having for the past six months. Her belief that my constant need to hold Drea is going to somehow make it impossible for her to sleep as she grows older, doesn't worry me. And even if it did, the feeling I get when I have her snuggled against my chest is well worth any frustration her sleeping patterns might cause later.

Because this grounds me.

Knowing she's here, that she's safe, the feel of her pressed against me, being able to look down and see Drew's face and that mop of curly hair, holding this tiny piece of him who is growing and thriving and is so loved by everyone around her, it helps me get through the hard days. The days when the guilt and the anger over how everything played out still get to me. When I have to rely on Ivy, Mom, and Dale to keep me from listening to the voices in my head that still love to try to seduce me to that place I never want to go again.

"She'll be fine, Ivy."

She sighs and stops digging in the bag. "You're not going to tell me why we're here?"

I shake my head, that tension moving from my spine

into my shoulders the closer we draw to the reason I've brought her to the museum today. "It's a surprise."

Ivy scowls. "Yeah, yeah..."

"I know you don't like surprises."

But I wasn't about to tell her about this one.

I couldn't.

This is something that has to be *seen* and it needed to be perfect before I showed Ivy.

"Come on."

I lead her through the museum and toward the contemporary and modern art wing. She raises a brow as we pass into it because typically when we're here, we head straight for Prometheus. But before she can ask anything, the familiar click of heels sounds on the floors and Roxy approaches us from one of the side galleries that has a sign marking it closed.

A bright smile spreads across her face, her eyes lighting up. "There you are."

Roxy rushes over and pulls Ivy into a tight hug she returns, and I grin, as Roxy whispers something conspiratorially into her ear. Whatever it is makes Ivy laugh and shake her head.

The fact that those two have grown so close over the past several months makes me happier than words can express. Roxy has become almost like another member of the family—though, Ivy might be annoyed that she was in on all this and kept it from her again.

Roxy approaches me and pushes up onto her toes in her heels to peek at the baby. "I see my favorite girl is taking a nap."

I nod. "She's been out for a while."

"Well, that's lucky for you because otherwise, you know I'd be stealing her for a while."

Grinning, I lean in and place a kiss on Roxy's cheek. "I'll hand her over as soon as she wakes up, I promise."

Roxy winks. "I'll hold you to that." Somebody calls her name across the gallery, and she waves. "Sorry, guys. I have to go, but find me after, okay?"

"We will."

Ivy raises a brow. "After what?"

That same anxiety tightens my gut. "You'll see."

Her brow furrows, and her lips twist slightly. "Why does that sound so ominous?"

Chuckling, I shake my head. "I promise, it isn't."

At least, I hope not, because honestly, this could go one of two ways and I have no idea which one it will.

Months and months of planning have all lead to this moment, and keeping anything from Ivy has been weighing on me—even if it was for a very good reason.

I hope she sees it that way...

Ivy allows me to lead her toward the gallery marked closed, but before we reach it, I pause and wait for her to do the same.

"Please try to understand..."

She raises a brow at me in question. "Understand what?"

"Why I had to do this."

Her eyes narrow, unease filling her gaze. "Cam, you're scaring me..."

I hate those words.

The last time she said them, I blew up her entire world.

Even though so much time has passed since that night, the ripple effects of it still linger.

That agony sometimes return when we least expect it.

But somehow, we've found a way to keep swimming against the tide of anguish.

We've kept our heads above water and grown stronger by taking things a second, a minute, an hour, a day at a time.

And *this* is part of that process.

Something that's been a long time coming.

"Go in."

She cautiously steps around me, leaving the stroller near the entrance, and enters the gallery through the black drapes with me right behind.

Her steps falter.

Her mouth drops open.

Her eyes lock on the massive canvas hanging in the center of the space.

"Oh, my God, is that..."

I step up beside her, my gaze raking over the image I've spent hours staring at and have memorized. "Yes."

She makes a little strangled noise in the back of her throat, and I glance over at her, but she's fixated on the canvas where I first made love to her, the night she came to my studio and learned the truth about what happened at Mom's birthday party.

I dip my head low so I can brush my lips against her ear. "I call it 'Worshiping Ivy,' and it was too beautiful not to share with the world."

"Cam..."

I can't tell by the way she says my name, if she's angry

or not, and she doesn't even look at me, so transfixed by it that she stands completely still.

Several minutes tick by as she examines every inch of the canvas—the smears, the blotches, the handprints in the paint that tell the story of our first time together.

The longer I wait for her to say something, the harder my body trembles.

My grip on a still sleeping Drea is that only thing that keeps me grounded enough to wait Ivy out and give her the time and space to gather her thoughts.

When she finally turns toward me, her eyes are wet, barely restraining tears. But before she can say anything, her gaze finds something over my shoulder and she pushes past me to approach it.

I hold my breath as she studies the paintings lining the wall.

Each and every one of her.

Some that she's seen before, others that I've done in the studio when I went over to work and tucked away so that she wouldn't get a glimpse of them when she came over to see what I've been painting over the last several months.

She walks slowly, examining each canvas, and pauses in front of the one I did of her on the bed our first night together, and I know she sees the change I made.

"I figured since many of these were intimate, you wouldn't want your face to be shown, so I modified them slightly, but the originals are still at the studio."

In any where her identity might have been revealed, I've changed it to a partial profile or cropped the painting completely so no one will ever know that it's her unless she wants them to.

But it doesn't make them any less haunting or any less beautiful.

Ivy doesn't say anything as we slowly make our way around the gallery, viewing the nearly four dozen paintings I chose to be part of the collection.

The longer it takes and the more time that passes in her silence, the more anxious I become for her reaction.

She hates it.

She's angry.

I shouldn't have done this without asking her permission.

What the fuck were you thinking, Cam?

Drea lets out a little annoyed sound before resettling against my chest, and I rub my hand up and down her back softly as I follow Ivy. Giving her some space to gather her thoughts.

When we finally reach our starting point back at the massive canvas, Ivy turns to face me, tears sliding down her cheeks.

My gut twists violently. "I'm sorry. I know I should have asked your permission. I understand if you're mad. I shouldn't have—"

"No." She shakes her head, a soft smile forming on her lips. "I'm not mad."

"You're not?"

She lets out a little laugh. "God, no. I'm...honored and surprised and..."

"Surprised about what?"

Her gaze travels over the gallery walls. "Is this really how you see me?"

I narrow my gaze on her. "What do you mean? You know it is. You've seen the paintings I've done of you. Well, most of them."

"Yeah"—she nods—"I mean, I have, but not like *this*."

"Ivy..." I close the distance between us and securing Drea with one palm, grasp Ivy's chin in the other. "There isn't a good enough artist in the world to truly capture how I see you and how beautiful you are, but this is as close as I could get."

She pushes up and kisses me, her lips gliding across mine in a movement filled with love, pain, and sorrow, then presses her forehead to mine. "Thank you. This is a tremendous gift."

I swallow the lump in my throat. "There's more."

Falling back on her heels, Ivy's brow furrows. "More?"

"Something I should have done a long time ago..."

I incline my head toward the adjoining gallery. "I call this collection 'Red,' but the one in there is different."

Chewing on her bottom lip, she moves toward the next gallery.

I'm frozen in place watching her step inside—a combination of anxiety and the grief that still lingers keeping my feet from moving to follow her.

A muffled sob falls from her lips as soon as she walks in, and I squeeze my eyes closed against the burn of tears, trying to keep from falling apart completely while Drea is in my arms.

Snuggling her close, I force my eyes open and follow Ivy.

She stands in front of a half dozen paintings of Drew —the ones I've done over the last several months, trying to capture those precious memories I have of him. Moments when he truly displayed who he was for the whole world to see.

I step up next to her. "I call this collection 'Light.'"

Because that's what Drew always was for everyone he met.

He pulled me out of dark places too many times to count. Helped me find my feet. Encouraged me to go to art school instead of just putzing around at my studio. He always wanted what was best for me and everyone else around him, and he would bend over backward to do what he could to get them there.

Which is why I *had* to do this.

Ivy walks up to the first image, reaching out her hand.

She trails her fingertips across the paint as if he's standing in front of her and this is her chance to touch him one last time.

Her hiccup sobs echo in the small room, a fitting soundtrack for the moment she comes face to face with him again like this.

I might not have been there for *this* particular moment captured on the canvas, but I see it every day in the photo on the end table...

The pure, vibrant joy radiating from his smile as he spun Ivy in his arms on that beach after asking her to be his wife.

And I know she recognizes it even though it's only his face in the image.

She places her hand over his lips, whispering something I can't hear, and when she turns back to face me, I know what she wants without her even asking.

I close the distance between us and carefully hand Drea off to her. She pulls her in close, snuggling her face into the baby's dark hair and carries her over to the painting.

But I hang back.

This moment isn't for me.

It's for *them*.

The three of them.

And when she moves away from the painting to examine the others along the gallery walls, I stay behind her, explaining each moment from our lives together captured and why I chose it.

So many memories of him.

Each important in its own way.

Not just for me, but for Mom, who already came and saw both collections yesterday.

And especially for Ivy and Drea.

Even if Drew's daughter can't see them right now or appreciate their meaning, I'll continue to paint them because this is what I promised I would do—help her know her father.

The light to my darkness, my other half...

When we reach the end of the collection, Ivy finally turns to me and stares up with tears streaming down her face. "Thank you."

I dip my head to press a featherlight kiss over her lips. "You don't have to ever thank me for anything, Ivy. If anything, I should be thanking *you* for giving me *everything*, but most of all, for your forgiveness."

Something I never thought possible.

Yet, somehow, we've reached that place. Through pain

and anger, anguish and guilt, we found a way to each other.

She was my sweetest obsession, and I became her sweetest agony.

Through it all, Drew was the light that has shone in the darkness and guided us to this moment. And now that light shines with Drea, the brightest star in the night sky over the shore he loved so much.

I hope you enjoyed Cam and Ivy's story in The Sweetest Lie Duet. For more angsty and emotional contemporary romances, check out The Billionaires of New Orleans: The Hawke Family and the Lumberjacks in Love series.

The Billionaires of New Orleans: The Hawke Family begins with *Savage Collision*, FREE at all retailers: books2read.com/SavageCollision

Lumberjacks in Love begins with *Billionaire Lumberjack*, available at all retailers: books2read.com/ BillionaireLumberjack

To stay up to date on news, releases, and sales from Gwyn, sign up for her newsletter here: www.gwynmcnamee.com/ newsletter

ABOUT THE AUTHOR

Gwyn McNamee is an attorney, writer, wife, and mother (to one human baby and two fur babies). Originally from the Midwest, Gwyn relocated to her husband's home town of Las Vegas in 2015 and is enjoying her respite from the cold and snow. Gwyn has been writing down her crazy stories and ideas for years and finally decided to share them with the world. She loves to write stories with a bit of suspense and action mingled with romance and heat.

When she isn't either writing or voraciously devouring any books she can get her hands on, Gwyn is busy adding to her tattoo collection, golfing, and stirring up trouble with her perfect mix of sweetness and sarcasm (usually while wearing heels).

Gwyn loves to hear from her readers. Here is where you can find her:

Website: http://www.gwynmcnamee.com/

Shop: http://www.gwynmcnameeshop.com/

Facebook:https://www.facebook.com/AuthorGwynMcNamee/

FB Reader Group: https://www.facebook.com/groups/1667380963540655/

Newsletter: www.gwynmcnamee.com/newsletter

Instagram: https://www.instagram.com/gwynmc namee

Bookbub: https://www.bookbub.com/authors/gwynmc namee

Tiktok: https://www.tiktok.com/@authorgwynmc namee

www.ingramcontent.com/pod-product-compliance
Lightning Source LLC
Chambersburg PA
CBHW060949030726
47503CB00003B/793